Katie and the Kiwis

Wendy Williams

This book is a work of fiction. Names,
characters, organisations, places and incidents
are either products of the author's imagination or
used fictitiously. Any resemblance to actual
events is entirely coincidental.

Cover design by Amelia Broome

Edited by Eleanor Broome

For Eleanor and Amelia

My inspiration

CHAPTER 1

'Katie, this is for you.'

Katie's dad holds a rectangular parcel in his hands. It is wrapped in shiny, purple paper and there is a purple ribbon tied in a pretty bow. Katie takes the parcel with a nod of thanks and places it on her lap. She is sitting between her mum and dad in a row of red, plastic chairs which are bolted to the floor. It is late and the bustle of the airport departure lounge is making her head ache. She is in no mood for bribes and blackmail.

Because without a doubt, that's what this is.

It isn't Christmas and Katie's thirteenth birthday is still six months away. This is a 'come quietly' present, a 'don't make a fuss' present, and

Katie is having nothing to do with it.

'Aren't you going to open it, Katie?' asks her mum. 'It's for the flight.'

With a sigh, Katie unties the ribbon and pulls off the paper. She has already guessed what might be inside from the shape of the package and because it is what she asked for last Christmas but didn't get. In fact, it is what she has asked for every Christmas since she knew they existed, but Mum and Dad have always said they are too expensive.

Too expensive until it suits them, thinks Katie.

She stares at the iPad on her lap. She has always been able to imagine the joy and excitement she would feel if she ever got to have one of her own. Now, she just feels more than a little bit sick and there is a lump forming in her throat that tells her this is most definitely not a gift. It is a trade. A brand new iPad in exchange for life as you know it.

'It's all ready to go,' smiles her dad. 'Have a look.'

Katie opens the iPad and looks to her dad for the code.

'1504,' he says, 'but obviously, you can change it to whatever you want.'

Katie taps the numbers on the keypad and the iPad springs to life. Beneath the screen of icons, she can see that her dad has loaded a photograph. It is a photo she has seen many times before today. A timber house is sitting on top of a hill beneath a bright, sapphire blue sky. The house has a sloping red tin roof, large windows and a wooden deck that runs all around the house. Surrounding it are pretty gardens which give way to rolling pasture and behind, there is a wide river speckled silver from the sunlight.

Katie feels her insides become hollow and her stomach drops with a dull thud beneath her ribs. The picture shows Great Auntie Janet's farmhouse. Great Auntie Janet who has died and left her farm to Katie's mum and dad. The farm that they are about to fly to because no matter what Katie wants, her mum and dad are going to make a new life on that farm.

In New Zealand.

As Katie stares at the picture of her parents' dream she becomes numb. Her shocked brain shuts down, her body becomes rigid and her hands refuse to work. The iPad slips through her frozen fingers and clatters onto the hard surface of the airport floor. Katie does nothing to try and stop it.

'Katie!' shouts her dad as he bends to pick up the iPad from the floor where it has landed face down. He turns it over and Katie can see the cracks across the blank, black screen.

It is ruined. Just like Katie's life.

Thirty-six hours later Katie is walking through the door of the very house that caused her to drop the iPad.

'Katie, you need to go to bed. Right now.'

'Mu-um!' Katie's jaw drops open in disbelief. 'We've only just walked through the door and we haven't even had lunch yet. I'm twelve and a half years old and it's the middle of the day. I'm not going to bed now. What's wrong with you?'

Katie watches her mum do that thing where she closes her eyes and in one sigh manages to convey just how difficult she finds life as Katie's parent. Only her clenched fists give a hint of the superhuman control she is using to keep her temper. Despite more than a day and a night of travel, it is obvious to Katie that her mum has not forgiven her for smashing the iPad. Katie is certain that if planes had bedrooms she would have been sent to one of them. Without any supper.

'That's enough of your lip, Katie. We've been traveling for over twenty-four hours and your dad and I are both shattered. Let's get some sleep and we can sort things out when we've all had some rest.'

Unbelievable, thinks Katie. Now I'm getting the blame for her decisions. Yet again.

'It's not my fault you're tired,' snaps Katie, just managing to stop herself from stamping her foot. 'None of this was my idea. You're the ones who wanted to come here.'

'Enough!' Katie's mum's eyes blaze with anger and her voice has a quiver that makes Katie back off. 'We have been over this a hundred times and I am not in the mood to go over it again. We are in New Zealand and we are staying in New Zealand.

The quicker you get used to the idea the better.'

Katie's mum has placed her hands on her hips and Katie knows that there is no point arguing. Besides, what is there to argue about? There is nothing in New Zealand that she wants to do. There is nowhere she wants to go. And she doesn't have a friend on the whole continent. She isn't even sure there is anyone else living on the whole continent judging by all the empty roads on the way here. She turns on her heels and flounces to the room that is supposed to be her bedroom, slamming the door behind her with a crash that reverberates throughout the timber house. There is a faint shout from her dad that might have been a swear word.

Katie drops carefully onto the rickety camp bed and covers her eyes so that she can't see the tiny room that is empty apart from the camp bed and the rucksack that she carried with her as hand luggage on the airplane. Her suitcase is in the car but dad was too tired to bring it indoors. In any case, that mostly contains nothing more interesting than clothes and shoes. Everything else she owns is tightly packed into a shipping container which will be loaded at Southampton in a few days' time. With luck, Katie might see her belongings sometime within the next two months. Unless of course some rubbish storm washes the container overboard and everything she owns is already at the bottom of the ocean growing baby barnacles. Google says that four shipping containers a day fall off ships and sink. What's the betting theirs will be one of the containers that takes a swim?

Not that the container will be of much use to Katie if it does arrive. Katie's mum made her throw away, or give away, almost the entire contents of her childhood.

'It costs far too much to ship all this stuff to New Zealand,' her mum had said. 'Especially now you don't play with it. It's much better that it goes to the charity shop so that another child can get some enjoyment from it.'

Katie squeezes her eyes tightly shut behind her palms and thinks of the bedroom she has left behind in England. Was it only two days ago? She loved their flat in London. She loved her room even more. They lived on the twelfth floor and Katie could see across the rooftops to the winding River Thames. For her whole life, or at least as far back as she can remember, Katie had watched the world from her bedroom window and dreamed of what she would do when she was older. Mostly, it involved Katie standing on a London stage receiving a standing ovation for her amazing performance as the most outstanding young actress to tread the boards for decades. In her very wildest dreams there is even an Oscar for her movie debut.

But it isn't going to happen now. Not after her mum and dad have exiled her to the bottom of the world because her stupid mother has inherited a stupid farm from a stupid Great Auntie she has never even met. And why did it have to be in New Zealand? Godzone Country it is called. God Forsaken more likely. Go any further and you would be dodging icebergs and eating seal blubber.

Stupid.

Stupid.

Stupid.

Stupid Great Auntie for dying. Stupid Mum and Dad for coming out to Nowhereland to shovel sheep shit and stupid world for making kids do whatever their parents say they have to do.

It is so *unfair*. Katie feels rage build inside her until she wants to scream out loud, but it isn't worth the telling off that will follow. And it certainly won't change a thing.

And now here she is in an empty room, in an empty house in this empty land. Katie is angrier than she thought it possible to be.

She growls and sits up on the bed. She reaches down for her rucksack and begins to empty the contents onto the camp bed. There isn't much. A notebook, pencils and felt pens, a small wash bag with her toothbrush and toothpaste, a packet of wet wipes, some tissues, two paperbacks, both read, half a bottle of water and her childhood doll.

It is the doll that takes up most of the space in the rucksack and Katie had worried that her mum might see it and make her leave it behind, but it is the one toy that Katie has always loved. She sits cross-legged and unwraps the doll from its thin blanket. Katie has no idea why she christened the doll Baby Beasta when she was not even three years old. But the name stuck and the doll is the toy that Katie carried everywhere with her when she was small. Katie fiddles with the matted hair and strokes the doll's grubby sleepsuit which is worn shiny from years of love.

For a moment Katie hugs the doll tightly and wishes that she could be small again, safe in the London flat with her best friend living two floors below. Instead, she is thousands of miles away from everyone and everything she has ever known. She has left it all behind. Not just who she has been, but who she was going to be too.

Katie feels her nose tingle but she sniffs hard and tucks Baby Beasta into the sleeping bag on the camp bed. She will not cry. She will focus on working out how she can get back at her mum and dad and make them wish they had never come here. And if that doesn't work, she will find a way to get back to

London the minute she is old enough to get away.

She will never forgive them for this.

Ever.

Katie kicks the rucksack under the camp bed, ignoring the one item that remains inside. It is the smashed iPad that her dad gave her at Heathrow Airport. Stinking, rotten blackmail. Is her dad really such a moron that he thinks an iPad will make everything alright?

Katie stands up and peers out of the window set into the sloping roof. The sun is high and the distant mountains shimmer with heat like a newly set jelly. Closer to the house she can see endless grassy fields, straight-edged tracts of woodland and sheep. Hundreds and hundreds of sheep scattered across the grass like white spots on a dotty, green dress.

Katie narrows her London eyes to look for buildings.

Nothing.

Maybe some roads?

Nope, just the bumpy drive they bounced along on the way to the house which Dad proudly informed her was one whole kilometre long. Like she was supposed to be impressed.

Power poles marching across the landscape? No, none of those either.

She squints so hard her brow furrows.

Maybe just one person? Perhaps a shepherd to look after all those sheep?

With a shock that makes her stomach clench, Katie realizes that she really is in the middle of nowhere. There is nothing here at all. Not a living human soul. What the…?

What on earth is she going to do?

How will she get to school?

Where *is* school?

Is there anyone to hang out with?

Are there speech and drama classes?

A ballet school, maybe?

Heaven help her. She isn't just at the bottom of the world. She is at the bottom of a very deep, dark dungeon.

And she has no hope of getting out.

CHAPTER 2

Katie takes a deep breath and blows it out slowly. She feels fidgety and full of energy after being trapped in cars and planes and airport lounges for what feels like half her life. Plus, the shock of realizing that there isn't any sign of human habitation for miles has left a coldness in the pit of her stomach that makes her feel queasy and strangely claustrophobic. She can't escape because there is nowhere to escape to. The freedom of open spaces that mum and dad talked about is actually a vast, empty prison camp.

Katie feels the empty bedroom closing around her as if it wants to trap her. She has to get out. Her mum can get lost if she thinks Katie is going to stay here for the rest of the day.

It isn't as if Katie's parents bothered with her in London. They both worked long hours and Katie was given a key to the front door as soon as she reached double digits. Katie knew very well that she shouldn't have been left alone in the flat at ten years of age but she had never cared at all. She squeezes her eyes tightly shut and pictures her school which was literally just around the corner and she didn't even have to cross a road to get there.

Once home, there was always someone or something to watch from the window and she knew most of the people in her block. If she was ever lonely, which was rare, there were half a dozen doors she could knock on where she would be welcomed with a hot cup of tea and something scrummy to eat.

She has to get out of this room.

Katie tiptoes down the stairs which only creak a tiny bit. At the bottom is a short hall that leads to the front door where they came into the house.

The first door Katie chooses is a cramped cloakroom with a toilet and a washbasin just big enough to wash one hand at a time. There is a tiny window covered in cobwebs and a bunch of disgusting bristles on a stick that must have been a toilet brush when it was born. Katie is just about to turn away when she spots a small box on the window ledge.

It isn't a particularly attractive box. If anything, it looks rather dusty and moth-eaten but Katie's hand is drawn towards it. She feels a tiny shiver as she wipes away the cobwebs but isn't sure if it is excitement at what is hidden inside or the thought that there could be a tarantula nesting in there. With dozens of babies!

Even though her mum's slumbering form is tucked up in bed, Katie imagines a sharp, 'Katie, don't touch!' as if her mum were right beside her. She opens the box anyway but with her arms held as far away from her body as they will go. She peeps inside. She is expecting to find jewelry. Perhaps there will be diamonds or something equally shiny and valuable that she will be able to sell on eBay towards a plane ticket home. Instead, she finds a cream-coloured carving lying in a bed of crushed, green velvet. It is a flat, curved shape, similar to a gigantic fish hook, but engraved all over with intricate, swirly patterns.

Katie gently removes the carving from the box and holds it in her hands. She couldn't explain the feeling if she tried, but the carving snuggles into her palm as if it belongs there. Its touch against her skin is as familiar as that of her childhood doll. It's as if she knows this hook. Katie strokes its surface which is smooth on one side, but irregular on the carved side. Threaded through a small hole at the top of the hook is a knotted string of black thread.

Katie lifts it over her head and lets the carving lie warm against her chest.

It feels special and precious.

This, she will keep.

Katie's hip is pressed against the wash basin and she is suddenly aware that she is squashed into a tiny cubicle that smells of drains and is probably home to a large percentage of New Zealand's bug population.

As she backs out she suddenly imagines giant

shutters slamming down around the house and trapping her. Is this what claustrophobia feels like? As if she is cut off from the rest of the world? What if she gets trapped? Her friends from home will wonder where she has gone but will never be able to find any trace of her. The fear that Katie has been holding in check since the day she knew she was moving erupts from her insides like some alien monster. It curls around her body and begins to slowly crush her ribs.

Katie is disappearing. She no longer exists in her old life. And no-one knows her in this new one. She is probably already forgotten. And might soon be invisible.

'Katie? Katie who?'

'Oh, you remember. That girl that went off to New Zealand.'

'Whatever.'

It's like I don't exist, she thinks.

It's bad enough being taken away from home when you don't want to leave. Especially when everyone is telling you how wonderful it's going to be. But with every new discovery Katie makes, the bad is becoming worse and Katie hasn't the first idea how she is going to survive in this wilderness as a nothing and a no-one.

The atmosphere inside the hallway is stifling and Katie can feel a fine sheen of sweat beginning to spread over her face. Abruptly, she lurches towards the front door and scrabbles at the handle with clumsy hands.

She really has to get out.

She tugs as hard as she can and the door flies open making Katie stumble back against the dusty wall.

Once through the doorway, Katie takes the three steps in one giant leap and lands crouched on the gravel panting with relief. What on earth is happening to her? Katie gulps huge lungfuls of air which is fresher than the air inside the house, but it's still warm and humid. Katie is grateful for the shorts and T-shirt that her mum insisted she change into at their stopover in Los Angeles.

She stands up and looks around as her breathing gradually returns to normal. The garden is jammed with trees, shrubs and flowers all shoved together and interrupted only by small squares of thick, patchy grass. Katie looks at the flowers with disinterest. They didn't have a garden of their own in London and these days the parks were somewhere for Katie to meet her friends and lie on the grass gossiping.

This spiky grass looks as if it will be very uncomfortable to lie on. Then there is the issue of not having any friends. And there is nothing and no-one to gossip about anyway.

Unexpected tears begin to trickle unchecked down Katie's face. They are tears of total despair. It is obvious that her mum and dad don't care about her one bit. All they care about are themselves and what they want to do. As long as they are happy, it doesn't matter what Katie wants. They haven't even bothered to ask her. Even now they have gone to sleep and left Katie shut up in her bedroom.

Well, that's what they think.

A sudden idea stalls Katie's tears and a tiny bud of excitement begins to bloom inside her. They don't care, so why should she? No-one is here. Nothing is here. Katie realizes she can do exactly what she wants. And right in front of her is a well-worn path that curves around behind a clump of towering hydrangeas. They are taller than Katie and will hide her so effectively from her mum and dad that they will think she is lost.

Oh my days! Wouldn't that just serve them right?

And that is her only thought. To sneak off and to hide. Just for a bit. Just long enough for her parents to really worry.

How was Katie to know that she would end up caught up, tied up and riding in the back of a Police car?

CHAPTER 3

The house and garden sit high above the river and as Katie sets off along the narrow path it begins to drop away steeply. She guesses that the path must lead down to the water and she feels a tight ball of excitement form in her tummy at the thought that she will be the first of her family to see it.

The dusty path twists and turns between the huge hydrangeas which are so tall they spill petals onto Katie's head like confetti at a wedding. She knows that she shouldn't really be wandering off and she knows that when her mum and dad find out they will be really angry with her. Well, so what? After all, it is their fault she is here in the first place. And Katie is determined to teach them a lesson.

Now and again, Katie has to clamber over

huge rocks stuck across the path which make deep steps so that her legs dangle for a moment before they hit the ground. In one place she lowers herself from a massive rock and hangs from her arms so she can drop onto the ledge below. The soil is sandy and dry and when she lands a small puff of dust coats her trainers and turns them orange. Her temper makes her want to stomp down the path but the ground refuses to let her and she finds that concentrating on keeping her footing helps her sour mood to improve just a little.

In the end, it doesn't take Katie long at all to reach the end of the path where she finds herself standing on the bank of the river which close-up, looks very wide and pretty scary. There are leaves and small branches being swept along in the current and because the water is clear, she can see wide patches of green weed covering the bottom of the river. Even though the river looks frightening, Katie is hot and sticky and the thought of dangling her feet in the cool water is much too tempting to ignore.

Right in front of her is a small, wooden jetty that she thinks looks just like an upturned picnic table.

Katie edges forward and carefully puts one foot on it to test its strength. There is a small creak, but it seems solid enough so she edges forward and sits down next to the criss crossed legs that stick up into the air like a dead sheep. She slips off her trainers and lets her feet slide into the deliciously cool water.

Katie closes her eyes against the sun and splashes her feet to and fro making a sparkling froth. For that short time, London, parents and home are all forgotten. Katie's only focus is the sound and feel of the water against her skin.

Then a noise comes from behind Katie which makes her freeze. It's the same sound that she had made herself when she pushed through the hydrangeas a few minutes ago, a sort of scrape, a rustle, and a small thud.

Then silence.

Something or someone is following her.

Apart from her mum and dad, she hasn't seen a living soul since their arrival on the farm.

Maybe it's an animal?

Katie's heart is just beginning to skitter inside

her chest when she hears another sound. Behind her the bushes are rustling. Or is it her imagination? Goosebumps pop up all over her arms and even though it is warm, she shivers.

Katie tries to remember whether her London Googling had said anything at all about wild and dangerous animals in New Zealand but the truth is, she doesn't know much about animals at all. Her dad had taken her to the zoo for her eighth birthday where she had been allowed to feed carrots to the giraffes, and there was sometimes dog poop on the pavements in London, but keeping pets in a flat was not an option, as her mum had told her so very many times.

What if it's a bear? Does New Zealand even have bears?

She stands up and turns quickly to look behind her just in time to see the bushes settling and sighing as if they are alive. Without realizing what she is doing Katie's hand goes to the carving that hangs around her neck. It feels warm beneath her hand and comforts her in a way that she couldn't possibly explain.

As Katie stands quite still listening, her knees trembling with fear, she hears something that reassures her, if only a little.

Breathing.

Human breathing.

'Hello?' she calls out in her bravest voice, which isn't a very brave voice at all.

Silence.

There is no reply to her question but Katie sees the branches in front of her quiver. She looks down towards the ground and sees a muddy, shoeless foot peeping out from the base of the bush.

Katie is relieved to see that it isn't much larger than her own and she takes a brave step forward.

'Who are you?' she asks.

'None of your beaky nose business,' is the reply.

Irritation wipes away Katie's fear. Even though she hates the stupid farm, it belongs to her mum and dad now and Katie feels affronted at the defiance in the stranger's voice.

'It *is* my business actually. This is my family's

land and *you* are trespassing.'

'Oh, so you're the new pommie, eh?'

'The what? What's a pommie?'

'Someone that comes from Pommieland. Pomgolia. The Pakeha's Motherland.'

Katie is exasperated. 'What on earth are you talking about?'

'I am talking about a Pakeha putting her Pommie toes on my jetty.'

Katie is bewildered. The voice sounds like a boy's and has a strange accent which she guesses must be New Zealand but she isn't completely sure. Whatever it is, she is struggling to understand a word it is saying. But even though she feels that she is on the back foot in the conversation, she is still cross. Her next words are snapped out.

'I don't know what on earth you're talking about but you had better get out of that bush because my dad will be down here in a minute.'

Of course, that is a lie. Katie's dad has the ability to sleep through a thunderstorm while in a tent and there is no hope of him appearing any time soon.

The idiot in the bush doesn't know that though and with a rustle of leaves, the boy steps out and reveals himself.

He is taller than Katie and has dark skin, black hair and brown eyes. They stare at each other in silence. Katie has her hands on her hips not knowing how much she looks like her mother. The boy leans on a pair of wooden oars, slouching with disinterest.

'Who are you?' asks Katie.

'Rangi.'

'Pardon?'

The boy curls his top lip. 'Rangi. You got cotton wool in your ears or what?'

'Rangi?'

'That's what I said.'

Katie sighs. 'Yes, I got that. But where have you come from?'

'I'm your next-door neighbour.'

Katie is bewildered. Where was next door? She had looked out of her bedroom window and there wasn't a house to be seen for miles.

'We don't have a next door,' she states firmly.

She is very keen to try and regain the upper hand in this conversation but feels like she is losing. 'We live in the middle of nowhere.'

Rangi sniggers. 'You still got neighbours. Everyone does. Even if it's only the ocean. Yours is just a bit more of a hikoi, eh.'

The sentence is spoken like a statement but the boy's voice goes up at the end and with the addition of the 'eh' it sounds like a question.

'What's a hikoi?'

'A walk,' he says and shakes his head as if in despair. 'You don't know much, do you?' He is looking Katie up and down with what looks suspiciously like a sneer.

Katie is even more annoyed now. Who on earth does this boy think he is?

'That's a bit rude,' she retorts.

Rangi shrugs. 'Seems like the truth to me. No need to get hosed off.'

'I am not hosed off, whatever that means. And I bet I know a lot more than you do.'

'Like what?'

Katie hesitates at first, thinking of the subjects she loves at school but this kid in front of her doesn't look like he would be impressed by her marks in Maths. His thick, black hair looks like it hasn't been combed ever and it is sticking out in every direction but down. The rest of him isn't any better. He is wearing a baggy T-shirt with a torn neck and an even baggier pair of ripped shorts that stop at two muddy knees above a pair of bare feet. She thinks he looks like an orphan from Oliver Twist.

Katie huffs. 'I know London like the back of my hand,' she says.

'Not much call for that round here,' he smirks.

She is pulled up short by the truth in his words. She is properly fed up now.

'I think you are the rudest boy I have ever met.'

'We've all got to be good at something.'

'And I suppose you think you're funny too?'

In response, a huge grin spreads across the boy's face and Katie has the feeling she has been outwitted. Is he goading her? Has he deliberately provoked her to get a reaction and has she been stupid enough to get caught out? She takes her hands from her hips and smooths down her T-shirt. She is at a loss to know what to say or do. She is annoyed that some trespasser is calling her names and being rude, but at the same time, this is the first and only person she has met since arriving in New Zealand. He looks about her age and there is a very good chance they will end up at the same school. She has a million questions that she would like to ask.

All the time that Katie is thinking and letting her confusion and annoyance wash over her face, Rangi is leaning on his oars and watching Katie as if he has nothing better to do with the rest of his life. It occurs to Katie that he is probably quite interested in her too. Even if he is the rudest boy on the planet, and before this last thought is fully formed in Katie's mind, Rangi confirms it.

'Boy, you're white,' he says.

'And you're brown,' Katie retorts. 'So what?'

'That's cos I'm tangata whenua,' he says, and he pushes out his chest with pride. He is actually quite a bit taller than Katie, even in his bare feet, and she has to look up at him.

'And I can barely understand a word that comes out of your mouth,' she says.

'Baarr-ly understaand,' Rangi replies, trying to mimic Katie's accent, which normally would have upset her but he sounds so much like the Queen she has to suppress a giggle. That makes Rangi look even more pleased with himself.

'So what's tangata whenua?' she asks.

'People of the land. I'm Te Arawa.'

'I still don't know what on earth you're talking about.'

'My iwi. My tribe,' he says proudly. 'My ancestors landed at Maketu, just up the coast. There's a statue there to mark the landing place of the waka.'

'Is that a boat?' Katie guesses.

'It's a Maori canoe. How come you don't know anything?'

'Maybe because I only just got here today,'

'Ah yeah. From Pommieland.'

'From England.'

'Same difference. So, what've you come here for?'

'Because my Great Auntie Janet died and left my mum her farm.'

'Ka Rawe! Awesome!' says Rangi. 'You must be stoked.'

'What do you mean, stoked?'

Rangi's forehead wrinkles up like a piece of corrugated cardboard as if he is puzzled or trying to decide something. Maybe he is trying to remember whether Great Auntie Janet had a boiler. But if she didn't have one, how could it be stoked?

Rangi looks pleased as if he has just got the answer to a really difficult puzzle.

'You must be rapt.'

Wrapped! Wrapped in what? Tin foil, birthday paper, a warm blanket on a frosty night?

'You say some very peculiar things, Rangi.'

'Pee-qu-li-a,' he repeats, mimicking Katie again. She thinks that he actually sounds quite good.

'No, it's pee-qu-li-ah!' she replies. Then they both laugh and the tension is broken a little, even though Katie still doesn't like Rangi very much at all. But if he is the only human for miles around, she might as well get some local knowledge while she has the chance.

'What's your name?' Rangi asks.

'Katie.'

'Katie,' he nods, but he pronounces it 'Kay-D'.

'No, Katie,' she repeats, 'K – T.'

'Kay-D,' he says again. But Katie decides she actually likes the way he says it so she doesn't correct him again.

'What's that mean?' Rangi asks.

'I don't know,' Katie answers truthfully. 'It's short for Katherine. That's all I know. Like the future Queen of England, but with a 'K' not a 'C'.'

And that was the truth. She had never given any thought whatsoever to the meaning of her name.

'You should Google it,' Rangi says, 'find out.'

I probably should too, she thinks, although I expect I would get a billion matches for Prince William's wife.

'Well, what does Rangi mean?'

'Sky or heaven, but most times mum calls me Raru.'

'Why? What does that mean?'

'Trouble. She says I annoy her and she calls me Raru. That's when I know it's time to go and get lost till she's cooled down.'

'Is that what you're doing now?'

He shrugs. 'Maybe.'

'How old are you?' she asks.

'Almost thirteen.'

'Hey! Me too.'

'Awesome!'

'So where's your house?'

He points vaguely behind his head where there is nothing to be seen but the bush.

'Just down river. You can come visit, eh?'

Why was he saying 'eh' at the end of every sentence? It made everything sound like a question. Katie is just about to question him on that when he gallops off into the bush waving for her to come with him.

With nothing better to do, she grabs her trainers and follows.

Katie's mum had told her to never go off with strangers. But that was before she had taken Katie to a whole country full of them. So what was Katie supposed to do? Go and listen to her dad snoring or go and have an adventure with her new friend Rangi?

No contest.

CHAPTER 4

Katie is not particularly worried about getting left behind, but the truth is, she has nothing better to do so she pulls on her trainers and hurries after Rangi. Once she is actually in the bush, it isn't as difficult to get through as it looks. Most of the leaves and ferns are lovely and soft and easy to push through. Rangi seems very sure about the way and trots along quite happily in his bare feet.

After the invitation to 'come visit,' Katie assumes they are going to Rangi's house but she decides it would be wise to check.

'Where are we going?' she calls as she puffs after him.

Rangi ignores her and Katie is suddenly afraid that she might really get lost. Or if she is gone for too long, her mum might actually wake, find her gone and alert every police officer in New Zealand. Katie could just see the headlines now, *'English girl lost in her own back garden'*. Huh! Imagine starting a new school with a reputation like that, she thinks. She should really stay close to the house so that she can pop up unharmed. Only after her mum and dad have started to panic of course, but before they actually ring the Police.

It is going to be a fine balance.

The gap between herself and Rangi has widened and Katie increases her pace. 'Hey, wait!' she calls as she hurries to keep up.

He pauses to turn back with a cross look on his face. 'Ssssh!' is all that he says. Katie is just about to tell him to get lost if that is how he feels when he stops so suddenly that Katie comes close to bumping into his back.

Katie can see that they are back on the river bank, only now they are at a proper jetty. It is solid and well-built and nothing like Great Auntie Janet's upturned picnic table. Katie spots a cute little wooden boat tied to a tall post. It looks like one of the boats that dad had hired once in Hyde Park to row Katie and her mum around the lake. Except this one is much smaller and painted a really nice blue. Rangi is busy untying the rope.

'Is this yours?' Katie's dad often says that she is the bomb at asking the obvious.

'Yeah, get in.' Rangi speaks as if he expects Katie to obey him without question. He doesn't know who he's dealing with, she thinks.

'How do I know you can even drive that thing?'

'Row,' he snorts. 'You row a boat.'

Katie knows that but for some absurd reason, she doesn't want Rangi to know she knows. For goodness sake, he might think she is actually interested in boats when London's tube map and the bus timetable are the full extent of her interest in forms of transport.

If she is hoping to annoy him, she has failed. He shrugs in a very indifferent and annoying way.

'Please yourself.'

Katie sighs. Her parents are likely to be asleep for hours and Katie can't face the thought of going back to Great Auntie Janet's house. She has two options. She can spend the rest of the day huddled beneath a hydrangea bush or she can do something that might be a tiny little bit interesting. Irritating and annoying as this boy is, he is present, he is local and he can probably answer some of the questions buzzing around inside her head about life here.

'Where are you going?' she asks again.

Agh! If he shrugs like that just once more Katie is going to storm off. Her head says she should slap him hard across the face but she has the feeling that if he hit her back she would come off worse.

'Get in if you're coming,' he says, over his shoulder, 'but you've gotta be real quiet.'

'Yes, but where are we going?'

Rangi rolls his eyes but Katie pretends not to notice.

'Up river. There's been some funny stuff going on and I'm off for a look-see.'

Katie hesitates for just a second, then climbs

into the little boat which bobs in the water so that she over-balances and sits down with a thump on a wooden plank that stretches across the width of the boat. If the blue boat lives here, at this jetty, then it has to come back here, she thinks. Katie knows that she can easily find her way back to the house from where they are. A short row on the river will actually be quite pleasant on such a hot day.

Even then, before they have gone anywhere at all, Katie knows that what she is doing is a bad thing. Even though Rangi seems okay-ish and he is her new neighbor and Katie is bored and cross, she knows that she shouldn't be going off with him. But right at that moment, she is still so angry at mum and dad for bringing her out here, at Great Auntie Janet for dying and even at New Zealand for being at the bottom of the world, that she doesn't care one jot. She just holds on to the sides of the little boat and waits for whatever is going to happen next to actually happen.

It wasn't at all what she expected.

CHAPTER 5

Rangi sits down opposite Katie. The boat is so small that their knees are almost touching. Katie compares her pink and shiny kneecaps to Rangi's brown ones. She can't tell if the colour is his skin or dried mud. He continues to ignore Katie as he tidies away the rope, fits the oars and begins to row.

That suits Katie. Once they are underway, she is quite happy to sit there and watch the riverbank drift lazily by. It is cooler down on the water and if she keeps her eyes focused on the river and not on the surrounding landscape, Katie is able to pretend that she is back in England.

Of course, Rangi has to interrupt her thoughts.

'Would you like a lolly?' he asks.

Katie's mouth waters at the thought and she

imagines the taste of orange or strawberries in her mouth. Maybe even lime.

'Yes please.'

He reaches under his seat with one hand and hands Katie something that looks like fish-shaped chocolate then resumes rowing.

'What's this?' she asks, examining it curiously.

'Chocolate fish.'

'Don't you have any lollies then?'

'That is a lolly.'

'No, this is chocolate. A lollipop is a hard sweetie on a stick.'

'That's a Chuppa Chup.'

'Is it?' was all she can think of to say. She isn't one hundred percent sure what they are actually talking about but it doesn't seem to be strawberry flavoured lollipops. Or any lollies come to that. Katie is a bit confused and stares at the chocolate fish thing while she tries to work it out.

'Don't you want that?' Rangi asks. 'It'll melt if you keep fiddling with it.'

Katie does want it. She is hungry and who doesn't love chocolate? She bites down hard expecting solid chocolate only to find her teeth snap together in what turns out to be a pillow of pink marshmallow. Boy, it's good. Katie chews with relish and even lets out a little sigh.

Rangi nods. 'I've got loads more under here if you're that hungry.'

He is rowing hard out now and they have already gone quite a long way up the river. Katie likes the noise that the oars make as they swoosh through the water and the way the water drips from their ends when they are lifted up into the air. Rangi is really good at rowing for someone who is twelve and Katie is about to tell him so but decides she will save that one till later. She doesn't want to make him any more big-headed than he already is.

But he is actually so good that she decides she will tell him after all.

'You're a really good rower.'

He smiles, showing a row of perfect white teeth. 'I'm on the water every time I can get away from mum's chores. Fishing's my favourite. But I haven't had much chance to catch fish lately with all this funny stuff going on.'

'What funny stuff?'

Katie can see that they are rowing past Great Auntie Janet's house now and the bedroom windows wink above the treetops. Let them rot, she thinks.

'There's been some hard case boat coming up here. Big flash thing, but going real slow. Comes up river about this time then heads off down again at dawn.'

'Why is that funny?'

'Them hard case power boats don't hang about, eh. They go flat tack. Give it heaps. They like to make real big waves. If they wanted to take all day they'd have one of these, eh.' And he shrugs to indicate his little rowboat.

'I suppose so,' Katie agrees. What he is saying seems to make some sense. But she still isn't sure where they are going or what they are going to do when they get there. It is slightly worrying to think that she has left home to row up a strange river, with a strange boy, in a strange boat, in a strange land.

'Has the big boat been today?'

'Yeah, it has too,' says Rangi. 'I watched it go past this arvo. Just before you came clomping down to the river bank.'

Katie is affronted. 'I don't clomp!'

'Well, you don't do quiet very well.'

'I wasn't trying to,' she retorts. 'What is it with you about quiet anyway? There is no-one around for miles.'

'There are the big fellas on that fancy boat.'

'How big?' asks Katie, a little worried now.

'Big enough. But it ain't the big fellas that bother me. It's their big guns.'

CHAPTER 6

'Big guns! Are you kidding me?'

A jolt of fear shoots through Katie and makes her grab the sides of the boat.

Rangi shakes his head and carries on rowing as if he has done nothing more than offer Katie another one of his lollies or sweeties or whatever the stupid fish are called. Katie's head is whirling with the words she has just heard but which her brain is struggling to make sense of. Big guns are in movies and on the telly. They aren't in real life.

'Hang on one minute. You're telling me that we're following a boat carrying big men with big guns?'

Katie's voice sounds funny in her ears, all

high-pitched and squeaky. Was this a joke? Or a dream?

Rangi is still rowing.

'Will you STOP!'

Rangi shushes her crossly but he does stop rowing and rolls his shoulders as if they are sore.

'Do you want them to hear us?' he asks in a whisper.

'No, of course, I don't. I want to know why we are going anywhere near them. Why aren't we going to fetch help or call the Police or something?'

Rangi sighs and the sound is very like the noise Katie's mum is so fond of making when Katie annoys her. It makes Katie feel very young and very silly. Rangi raises his hand to tell Katie to wait and starts to row again but this time he turns towards the bank of the river where he pulls the boat in beneath the welcome shade of a large tree.

Once they have stopped, Rangi fishes under his seat and produces a bottle of water, which he offers to Katie. She drinks her fill, wipes her mouth with the back of her hand and hands the bottle back.

Rangi also drinks before he speaks.

'So, I guess I haven't told you everything, eh.'

Katie wants him to hurry up but she bites her tongue and makes herself wait. 'I guess you haven't.'

Rangi chews his bottom lip for a moment, then starts to speak.

'I've been seeing these hard case power boats coming up river for weeks now.'

'So you said.'

'Yeah, but big boats don't come up here. There's a speed limit on the rivers and there's nothing up here. A big boat might come up here once out of curiosity, but they wouldn't keep coming back. Not day after day. And at the same time too.'

'Except this one does.'

'Except this one comes up, stays overnight and leaves early next morning.'

'So?'

'So, give me a break. Don't you think that's kinda weird.'

Given that Katie has never seen a big boat and hasn't the faintest idea what a hard case boat is, it is difficult to form an opinion on what is weird and what isn't.

'They could be camping?'

'Ya reckon?'

'Well, I don't know, do I? I've haven't been in this stupid country for a day yet and I'm in a boat chasing baddies with guns.'

Rangi grins.

'Good, eh?'

Why is he so exasperating?

'No, not good, Rangi. I would like you to take me back now.'

'If you want to go back now Kay-D, you're gonna have to swim.'

Katie sits up straight in the boat. 'Now look here.'

'Now look nothing. I haven't rowed all the way up here to let you dangle your pretty little fingers in the water.'

'I have not dangled...'

'Not the point. There is something I need to do and you chose to come with me.'

'I don't remember being given a choice.'

'Everybody has a choice. Get in the boat. Don't get in the boat. You got in. End of.'

Katie is totally flabbergasted. 'This is crazy, Rangi. There are men with guns!'

Rangi shrugs. 'Most families in the bush keep a rifle. My dad has one. He takes me possum shooting sometimes.'

'Possum…what?'

'Possum shooting.'

Katie is horrified.

'You and your dad shoot innocent wild animals?'

'You really don't know anything do you?'

'You can't kill animals like that.'

'Kay-D, possums don't belong here. They were brought over here for their fur and now there are thirty million of them. They're pests. They eat everything: leaves, flowers, fruit, eggs, birds, insects, snails. You wait till your mum gets her veggie patch going. It won't last long round here. Possums will be at it just as soon as her back is turned.'

Katie tries to imagine about thirty million possums and wonders what that might look like. She imagines a Pied Piper figure followed by a plague of very large, very furry rats eating everything in sight. Katie thinks of the book her mum gave her about New Zealand and remembered the chapter on wildlife.

Katie was too cross to bother reading the whole book but she had read that one chapter. She had liked the pictures of the cute kiwi birds with their long beaks and soft feathers.

'Do they eat kiwis?'

'Yep. Eggs, chicks, and birds. I think they spit out the feathers though.'

'Well, maybe,' suggests Katie, 'the men on the boat are shooting possums.'

'Not in the same place every night, Kay-D. Doesn't work like that.'

Katie slumps on her wooden seat. There is so much to learn about this new country and she suddenly wishes she had taken the trouble to find out more before she came. *Everything* is different.

She narrows her eyes at Rangi. 'Good job.'

'What's a good job?'

'The way you just managed to distract me from men with guns to pesky possums. Very clever. And don't you dare smirk.'

Rangi simply picks up the oars and starts to row again. 'We need to get going. We've still got a way to go.'

There is nothing for Katie to do but sit. She has no intention of swimming all the way back to the jetty and despite the fact that she is seriously scared, she has no choice but to sit tight and trust. And curse her stupidity for wandering off when she could be safe on the camp bed with Baby Beasta and a shattered iPad.

The camp bed in the silent and empty room.

Katie groans out loud at the thought and covers her face with her hands.

'You packing a sad?' asks Rangi.

Katie shakes her head and uncovers her face.

'What sort of God Forsaken Country have I been brought to?'

Rangi regards her with curiosity. 'You don't

want to be here, eh?'

'You think, Mastermind?'

'Why not? It's so cool here. England gets rain and ice and snow, all the time.'

'Slight exaggeration. It's not *all* the time.'

'It's pretty crowded over there.'

'There is masses of stuff to do.'

'There's masses to do here, Kay-D.'

'Like chase big men with guns.'

'That's just today, eh?'

'It should be never. And I shouldn't be here. I don't belong here.'

'So, why'd you come?'

Katie glared at Rangi. 'Why do you think? I'm twelve years old. I have to do what my parents say and they said we were coming here. I didn't have a choice.'

'Didn't you talk about it?'

'Are you kidding me?'

Katie thinks back to the day that her parents broke the news and before she can stop herself the whole story comes pouring out.

Rangi rows steadily up the river and listens.

Katie tells her story.

CHAPTER 7

'Ok, so let me get this right. Your Great Auntie Janet dies and leaves her block to your mum. Your dad decides he wants to be a farmer and leaves his job in a bank. Then, you leave home and are dragged onto a plane to New Zealand?'

'That about sums it up.'

'No wonder you're packing a sad.'

Katie isn't sure if she wants sympathy. It is making her feel sorry for herself and she is determined that she will not cry in front of this boy.

She tries one of Rangi's shrugs.

'So, what are you gonna do?'

'Get back home as soon as I can.'

Rangi nods. 'Guess that's what I would do too.'

'It's just going to be a really long time to wait.'

'So, I guess it's just by chance that you ended up here?'

'Yes. Chance and my Great Auntie Janet dying.'

Rangi shakes his head. 'No. I mean that's why you're *here*. In my boat.'

'What do you mean?'

'Can't think of any girl I know who would take off with me like you did just now. You got some guts, girl.'

Katie feels a rush of pride at the compliment which fades as soon as she remembers exactly where she has taken off to. And now that the ice is broken between them she wants to know exactly where they are going.

'So, tell me what's going on. Properly tell me.'

'I've followed these guys before,' explains Rangi. 'More than once. They moor their big boat near a side creek and take off in a small dingy.'

'And have you found out where they go?'

'Sure have.'

'And?'

'I think,' says Rangi, 'that they're poaching Kiwi birds.'

'*What*? Poachers. Are you sure?'

Katie knows from her book that kiwis are very cute and very, very shy. 'Aren't kiwi birds endangered?'

Rangi nods. 'Not many eggs hatch and when they do, they get eaten by dogs, cats, possums, and stoats. They can't fly away, see. Best they can do is hide in the bush. If we're not careful, they'll all soon be gone.

'Oh. That's so sad.' Katie feels her eyes tingling at the thought of the cute birds with their long beaks being murdered.

'So, why are they being poached?'

Rangi shrugs. 'Not sure I know, Kay-D. Maybe for their feathers. Maybe for private zoos. It's against the law to take them out of New Zealand and I can tell you, these guys ain't conservationists.'

'So, you're going to stop them?'

Rangi nods. 'Sure gonna try.'

'So, what exactly did you see?'

'I followed the men to an old timber bush hut. There are a few still around. They're old as, and mostly falling down, but this one has been fixed up.'

'Did you get a look inside?'

'I didn't get near. There was a guy already in the hut and he came out with a dog so I scarpered before that mangy runt got my scent.'

Katie felt a shiver of excitement as she pictured a tumbledown hut, Rangi lying in the bush and a vicious, snarling dog. This was unreal.

'So, how do you know the men are poaching?'

'I heard the kiwis calling, eh.'

'What do they sound like?'

'It's a sort of high pitched warble. I could hear a male calling for a female and he just wouldn't give up so I think his wife was captured.'

Katie pauses to absorb everything Rangi has told her. She had been quite frightened when he had talked about men and guns and she is still scared, but the thought of the Kiwis being caught and sold or even killed breaks her heart.

While Katie is thinking about the cute Kiwi birds, she can't focus on anything else. Not London, or moving, or New Zealand or anything else at all other than what the poachers are doing. All she knows is that it is wrong and that she and Rangi can do something to put it right. She looks Rangi in the eyes.

'I'm in. Let's do this.'

CHAPTER 8

Rangi continues to row and Katie sits quietly, deep in thought. As the afternoon begins to creep towards the cooler early evening, Rangi has to stop for frequent rests. Katie wants to offer to row but she doesn't know how and isn't sure this is the time to learn.

As they round a bend in the river, Katie catches sight of a huge power boat moored next to the river bank. Rangi was right, she thinks. It does look odd stuck out here in the middle of nowhere. From what Katie can see, it also looks deserted.

'There,' she points.

'This is it. We're here Kay-D.'

Straight away Katie starts to feel nervous again, and despite the cooler air, she has to wipe her sweaty palms on her shorts. They turn into the small side creek and Rangi is forced to row with alternate oars as the river narrows.

As well as stealing the light and warmth, the approaching twilight is stealing some of her nerves and Katie is starting to feel a bit jittery. She is afraid as much about what they are going to find, as she is about being lost up a river on her very first day in New Zealand, with Rangi as the only witness. Rangi is her only witness because no-one else in the world knows where she is. And it occurs to Katie that if anything happens to them, they might never be found.

That would really teach her mum and dad.

Katie opens her mouth to share this thought but all she gets from Rangi is a loud, 'Sssh!' and a shake of his head.

He rows the boat right into the river bank so they are hidden by all the overhanging branches, tall grasses, and other green stuff.

Within a blink, Rangi is on the river bank tying the boat to the furry trunk of a palm tree.

'This is a ponga,' whispers Rangi, as he pats it. 'It's a New Zealand tree fern. The trunks float.

Remember that.'

He holds out his warm hand and Katie climbs out of the boat with as much care as she can manage. Her legs are stiff from sitting in the boat for so long and she stumbles as she steps onto the river bank. Katie thinks the water looks horrible and black in the shade of the trees and she definitely does not want to fall in.

Then Rangi raises his finger to his lips to indicate that Katie should be quiet as he sets off into the bush. Katie tries really hard to keep up with him and stay quiet. They aren't following any clearly defined path but Rangi seems to have a very good idea of where he is going. He pushes aside waist-high ferns and sidesteps pongas as if they are cracks in the pavement. Katie concentrates on trying to place her feet in Rangi's footsteps and not make any noise.

Then Rangi is gone.

Katie almost steps on him before she realizes he is lying flat on the ground in front of her. She drops down beside him and he points into the bush ahead of them.

There is a lot of greenery and for a minute Katie isn't sure where she is supposed to be looking but then she manages to make out the shape of a ramshackle shed. It isn't massive, probably the same size as a double garage and it seems to be made up of a patchwork of timber. Katie thinks it just looks like any old shed, but what does she know?

For a long time, they do nothing but lie still and keep watch. To Katie, the earth smells really lovely, mossy and mushroomy, and even though the temperature is falling she feels quite comfy snuggled into the earth. And the longer she lies there, the more she begins to hear too. There are buzzing insects, rustling leaves and even an owl hooting.

Rangi stiffens beside her and Katie raises her head to peer into the gathering gloom. She reaches for Rangi's hand and he squeezes hers back.

Katie can hear voices. As she watches, two men emerge from the shed and Katie can see their silhouettes against the trees. Each man carries a rifle over his shoulder and a large torch in his hand.

Katie drops her head down and finds herself

staring into Rangi's eyes.

'I have to get a look inside that shed,' whispers Rangi.

Where is his brain? thinks Katie.

'No!' she hisses. 'It's too dangerous. What if we get caught?'

'We won't,' he answers. 'We wait till they've gone.'

'How do you know they will go?'

'That's what they did last time. I think they go and check traps.'

'What if they've got the dog?' Katie asks.

'They'll take him,' says Rangi with such certainty that Katie has no doubt that this is exactly what will happen.

'And we'll stay downwind,' adds Rangi.

Katie's heart is beating so loud in her ears she is sure the men will be able to hear it.

'Let's just go and tell someone what we've found.'

Rangi shakes his head. 'What have we found Kay-D? An old settler's shed is all.'

'But the kiwis.'

'I *think* there are kiwis, Kay-D. I haven't actually seen them. What if I call the Police and they *are* just possum hunters? I need to get a real look. Then we can tell people.'

Katie sighs. She doesn't like it but she can see the sense in what he is saying. One quick look and they can be gone. No-one will even know they have been there.

Rangi becomes really still and quiet. Katie turns to look back at the shed. The men have indeed been joined by a large dog. The door to the shed is closed and just as Rangi has predicted, Katie sees the men set off into the bush with the dog trotting behind them. They wait until the bobbing streams of torchlight have faded away before Rangi stands up and holds out his hand to Katie.

Her heart is beating so loud she can hardly hear herself think and she is sure Rangi must be able to hear it too.

'Reckon it's time to take a look,' says Rangi.

Katie's chest tightens with panic and she grabs

Rangi's arm, pinching it hard so that he gasps before pulling her fingers away.

'You can't go over there. Please, Rangi.'

'Got to,' he says, 'or how will we know what's goin' on in there. Might be nothing, might be something. Either ways I gotta find out. Else all that rowing was a big waste of time.'

Katie realizes that if he goes to look inside the shed, he will leave her there in the dark. Alone.

'I'm coming too.'

'No!' Rangi practically hisses when he says it. 'You stay here. I know this bush and I can be quiet.'

Katie supposes this is his polite way of saying she will be banging around like a wild elephant.

'If you leave me here, Rangi, I will be terrified. And when I get frightened, I tend to scream.'

Of course that isn't true. Or at least Katie doesn't think so. If she thinks about it, she can't actually remember being truly terrified about anything before today. And even though she is quite frightened at this very moment, she knows full well that screaming will make things very bad indeed.

She watches Rangi watching her while trying to make up his mind. Then he points his finger at her. 'Not a peep,' he says.

Katie mimes zipping her mouth closed and presses her lips together to hide the smile that is trying to escape. Rangi turns away and begins to step carefully and quietly through the bush. Katie is almost surprised to find herself following him.

CHAPTER 9

Katie can see that it isn't far to the shed, but the daylight is fading fast and the dense bush thickens the gloom so that she has to concentrate on where she is placing her feet. She also has to keep reminding herself to breathe. Even though she is frightened, Katie is excited too. If only her London friends could see her now having a real adventure, instead of lying on the grass in the park making up their own. She doesn't think for a minute that anyone would believe her. She can barely believe it is real herself.

Katie sees Rangi flapping his hand indicating to Katie that she should stop. He stands motionless listening and Katie tries to slow her breathing so that she can listen too. As the sun sets the insects in the bush begin to hum and chirrup so loudly that Katie can barely hear anything else.

'What *is* that noise?' she whispers.

'Crickets,' replies Rangi. 'And Katydids.'

'What did I do?'

'Not you. Katydids are big green bugs. Listen. They are saying Katy did, Katy didn't, Katy did, Katy didn't.'

Katie listens carefully and she really can hear the chirruping bugs saying exactly that.

'That is so cool,' says Katie.

'It is,' whispers Rangi, 'but it's not cool that you are talking.'

Katie clamps her mouth shut but carries on listening to the bugs. She is thrilled that New Zealand has a green bug that shares her name and wants so much to see one.

Rangi turns and motions to Katie to follow him. They approach the shed from the back where there is a small window set quite low in the wall. Katie crouches down next to Rangi to peer inside but a piece of old sacking has been stuck to the window and there is nothing to be seen.

Katie's heart begins to thump again as they creep around the side of the shed to the door. Katie is surprised to see that it isn't locked but then she supposes the two men would not be expecting visitors in such a lonely spot.

Katie watches as Rangi opens the wooden door with great care and steps inside. Katie is right on his heels.

It is so dark inside that Katie has to stand still for a moment waiting for her eyes to adjust to the light and there is a musty, compost sort of smell. She can hear stirring and shuffling all around her and is just thinking of worrying about rats and possums when Rangi produces a tiny torch from the pocket of his shorts and shines it around the shed.

Katie gasps.

The shed is stacked from floor to ceiling with cages and each cage contains a Kiwi bird. In the centre of the shed is a rough wooden table with a pile of empty cages scattered underneath it. Katie can see that the floor of the shed is nothing more than trampled earth although there are imprints of wooden planks in the ground as if there had once been a proper floor.

'You were right, Rangi,' whispers Katie, clutching his arm. 'There are so many.'

'I so wish I wasn't right. Look at this. It's kino, so evil.'

As Rangi shines his torch around the shed Katie can see that the cages are barely big enough to contain some of the larger birds and although they are shuffling their feet and poking their long beaks into the straw, some of the larger birds are unable to turn around. Now and again a long beak pokes between the wires of the cages and snuffles in the cold air as if to try and work out who is there. The eyes of the birds glitter in the beam of light and Katie thinks it makes them look as if they are crying.

'They haven't got anything to eat or drink,' says Rangi. 'They'll starve if they're left here.'

Katie feels a lump in her throat as she looks at the beautiful birds trapped in their tiny cages. Tears are pricking her eyes and she rubs at them with the back of her hand.

'What shall we do, Rangi? Should we let them go?'

'If we let them go, the poachers will know that we've been here and they'll scarper. If they aren't caught, they will carry on. And there won't be any proof for the police if the birds are all gone.'

'What then?'

'We go back and get help. Quick as we can.'

Katie feels her insides twisting at the thought of the long boat trip back to the house and the poor, trapped birds left alone without food or water, but at the same time she badly wants to be out of the shed that is starting to feel too much like a coffin for the birds.

'What if they die before we get back?'

'I don't know how long they've been here Kay-D, but we can be back by sunrise. We'll be rowing with the current instead of against it and the police have power boats. We have to go and get help.'

Katie's mind is whirling. She wants to shout at Rangi for not telling an adult about his suspicions. She wants to open the cage doors and let all the little birds run free. But more than that, she wants the evil men that have done this to be stopped.

'Come on then, Rangi. Let's hurry.'

Rangi leads the way back to the door and he closes it behind him. Katie watches him switch off the torch and push it into his pocket. She knows that they have to hurry. The lives of the kiwis depends on them.

In the distance a dog barks.

Katie and Rangi stare at each other, their eyes wide with horror.

'They're coming back,' says Katie.

Rangi grabs her hand and pulls her into the bush. 'It's too soon. Come on, Kay-D. Fast as you can.'

But Katie pulls back on his hand. 'That's the wrong way,' she whispers. 'The boat is behind the shed.'

'So is that dog,' hisses Rangi, and he tugs hard so that Katie has no choice but to stumble after him.

Rangi forces a path through the bush, dragging Katie behind him. She can't see much of where they are going but in one short afternoon she has come to trust Rangi's sense of direction. Besides, she has no choice. She feels plants and vines tangling around her legs and she stumbles several times as she tries to keep up.

Just as Katie's lungs are starting to hurt, Rangi comes to an abrupt halt.

'Ok. This should do it. Let's listen.'

It is hard to listen at first with their panting breath but as the sun has now set, the crickets and katydids have stopped singing and the bush is quiet apart from an occasional hoot or animal call.

'Why did the men come back so quickly?' asks Katie.

'Who knows? Maybe they forgot something, or maybe they already had enough birds.'

'Will they follow us?'

'Not so far,' replies Rangi. 'But it doesn't mean they won't. If we're in luck they won't even know we're here. I guess it all depends on the dog. We need to get back to the boat, quick as.'

'But what if they're still in the shed?'

'We'll skirt round it, Kay-D. It will take us a

bit longer but we don't have a choice. We have to get back and we have to get help.'

Katie nods. More than anything in the world she wants to get out of the bush and back to civilization. Right now, that means Great Auntie Janet's house and Katie's mum and dad. How quickly things can change she thinks. 'Let's go then.'

'Just a few more minutes,' says Rangi. 'Let's make sure the coast is clear. Sit for a sec.'

They sit side by side with their backs against a ponga tree. Katie is tired now and her tummy growls with hunger. She wonders if her mum and dad are awake yet and if they have discovered that Katie is missing. She rests her chin on her knees and feels an overwhelming sense of stupidity and embarrassment. What on earth had she been thinking running off like this? Like it was going to make any difference to anything other than getting her a mega telling off and some outstanding punishment. She groans quietly.

Rangi pats her shoulder. 'It's ok, Kay-D, won't be long.'

Katie lifts her head to look at him. 'How on

earth do you stay so calm?'

That shrug again. 'Mum and Dad say I might be young but I'm showing signs of mana.'

'What's mana?'

'It's hard to explain to a Pakeha, which is you,' says Rangi. 'Mana is inherited but it can grow and shrink depending on how you live. It's about power and honour and respect. You earn it by doing the right thing. By caring for your family, for your tribe and for your land. You don't need to be told someone has mana. They just need to walk into a room and them being there is enough.'

'So, does mana make you brave?'

'Maybe. Helping the kiwis will make my mana grow. Catching and killing them would take away from my mana. But being boastful and big-headed will take away from it as well, so even if I felt brave I couldn't tell you.'

'It sounds quite complicated,' says Katie.

'I guess it seems that way if you haven't grown up with it.'

'Can women have mana?'

'Sure they can. Mana wahine. All mana comes from the gods and for women it comes from the Earth Mother and other female gods.'

'But...'

'No more questions for now, Kay-D,' says Rangi as he stands up. 'We have to get moving.'

Katie stands up slowly, her legs stiff from sitting on the now damp ground and she wishes she had some warmer clothes to put on. But sitting chatting with Rangi has calmed her and she is ready to move on.

'Ok. Really quiet now Kay-D.'

Katie nods and Rangi turns and begins to retrace their steps.

Once again, Katie has no idea at all where they are during their walk. She just follows. She is still tired, still hungry and still wanting to help the kiwi birds but once they are moving again she finds she has energy that she didn't know was there.

She settles into a rhythm of steps as she follows Rangi who is once again weaving around the trees and vines. Katie lets her mind wander back to the birds and worries about whether they will be in time to save them.

Without any noise or warning a dark shape steps out in front of them and grabs hold of Rangi. Katie has no time to think or react but Rangi's voice rings out clearly in the forest.

'Run, Kay-D. Run!' he shouts.

Katie runs for her life.

CHAPTER 10

As she turns away Katie catches a brief glimpse of dark shapes, and tangled limbs and hears a series of muffled grunts. She dodges to the left of the large human shape that is grappling with the smaller, skinny one and throws herself into the bush.

There is no time to think about where she is going or what she will do when she gets there. Katie's only thought is to put as much distance between herself and the poachers as possible. If there is any conscious thought at all in her head it is simply, 'get help.'

Her lungs scream for air and vines claw at her legs but Katie keeps on running. The moon is hanging high above the treetops and although the bush above her head is thick and dense, there are enough gaps in the foliage for Katie to be able to see a little of where she is going. She is glad that there doesn't seem to be any prickly English brambles to scratch her shins, but there are still plenty of creepers, fallen branches and knotted roots to trip her up and make her stumble and fall. Which she does, far more often than she would like.

But each time she stumbles, she wipes away her tears, pushes herself back onto her feet, and carries on.

By the time Katie is forced to stop and catch her breath she knows that she is hopelessly and completely lost. Any sense of direction that she may have possessed has been wiped out by her frantic dash through the New Zealand bush. She hangs on to a thick, black creeper that looks like electrical wire looped through the trees and bushes. She is shaking from head to foot and she sinks down onto her knees while she gasps and pants and wonders what on earth she is going to do.

Katie places the palms of her hands onto her burning cheeks and as her breathing slows, she begins to feel the sore spots on her knees where she has fallen and scraped away the skin. She tries to peer at them in the darkness to see if there is blood when a sudden movement behind her makes her gasp.

'Ssh!'

It is Rangi.

'Oh!' was all she says as she throws her arms around his neck in complete and utter relief. Rangi hugs her back then pushes her away to get a good look at her.

'You ok, Kay-D?'

'I am now you're here. How did you get away?'

'Walloped him.' Rangi makes a fist as if to demonstrate.

'But...' All Katie could think was that whoever had lunged at Rangi was very big and although Rangi said he had mana, his fist is looking pretty small.

'How?'

Rangi grins. 'It's not how hard you hit, it's *where* you hit. Hit the right spot and even a big fella will drop like a boar.'

'Oh.' Katie decides not to ask any more questions about the big fella. She is so happy to see Rangi, it doesn't much matter what he has done to get away.

'Are we lost?' she asks.

'Nah,' says Rangi. 'But it's going to be some hard yakka getting back to the boat. You sure can run for a girl.'

'Well, it's made me thirsty.'

'Yeah, me too. Here, have this.'

Rangi reaches up to the black cable and tugs hard. He pulls the long vine towards him until the end comes free from the bushes. Rangi breaks off the tip and hands it to Katie. 'Suck on that.'

'What is it?'

'It's called supplejack. Tastes a bit like celery but it's full of moisture. Only eat the tip though. The rest is tough as, eh.'

Katie looks at the end of the vine which reminds her of an asparagus tip. Rangi had found another vine for himself and is chewing his with relish. Katie tastes the very tip of the vine at first and as promised, it is moist and juicy. It is gone in seconds.

'Choice, eh?' says Rangi.

'Very choice. What now?'

'Back to the boat. But those fellas are looking hard for us now and they've got the dog.'

Rangi pauses and looks at Katie with such a serious face that her stomach goes cold. Katie knows from TV just how good dogs can be at tracking people.

'There's only one way in and out of this place,' says Rangi, 'and those fellas know that too. I'm not sure I can get us both away. We're going to need a plan.'

'What sort of plan?'

Rangi stares at Katie.

'Kay-D. Listen. You gotta do as I say.'

Katie nods and listens. And even though her heart sinks to her shoes, she carries on listening carefully. When Rangi is done, she nods once and says, 'Ok, let's go.'

They both stand up and Rangi raises his fist in a salute and says, 'for the kiwis.'

Katie raises her own fist and taps hers against Rangi's. She doesn't need him to tell her that it has no more strength than a well chewed piece of supplejack.

Because it is dark and because even in broad daylight, the bush would all have looked the same, the tramp back towards the little, blue rowing boat passes in a blur for Katie. Despite being tired, hungry and very, very scared, she is so focused on getting back to Great Auntie Janet's house that she is able to put one weary foot in front of the other without complaint. She even ignores her sore knees.

From time to time, Rangi pauses to check that Katie is ok, and each time she gives him a tired smile and a thumbs up.

When Rangi stops and turns towards her, Katie knows that they are almost there. Rangi points straight ahead. 'See the gap in the trees?'

Katie nods at the circle of light, clear sky.

'That's the stream. You'll need to follow it a ways to find the boat but keep going and you'll hit the creek. Follow the current to the big river then turn left and keep going.'

There was one major problem with Rangi's plan. 'I've never rowed before, Rangi.'

'You'll get the hang of it.'

'What if I don't?'

'Then the current will take you. But Kay-D.'

'What?'

He grins as he speaks. 'It will be a lot quicker if you row, eh.'

Katie nods. She feels hollow inside and the thought of being separated from Rangi makes her mouth go even drier, if that is possible.

'Are you sure about this, Rangi?'

As if in reply they hear a dog bark. 'They're still looking for us, Kay-D, and they won't give up until they find someone.'

'But they know there are two of us. Won't they keep on looking?'

Rangi takes Katie's hand and squeezes it. 'You know the plan Kay-D. One of us has to get away and fetch help. It's our only chance and it's the kiwis only chance. Why else are we here?'

Katie nods and with a wink Rangi turns and slips away into the bush. He is determined to act as a decoy so that Katie can slip away and fetch help. She moves quietly forward towards the water. She will not let Rangi down.

With the help of the lighter patch of sky, Katie is able to make out the outlines of trees and bushes and finds she is able to move at a good pace. She stops for a moment when she thinks she hears the dog again and what sounds like a man's voice, but she knows that she has to stick to the plan whatever happens. Rangi will distract the men and Katie will get to the boat, get away, get help and save the kiwis.

Suddenly she is there. The water shimmers like silver in the moonlight and Katie can see the outline of the ponga tree where they have tied the boat. Her heart lifts as she hurries towards it.

Except the boat isn't there.

The boat is gone!

Hot tears prickle Katie's eyes. She stands staring at the empty space where Rangi had left the boat and tries to work out what has happened to it. Was she in the right place? Yes. There were the trampled ferns by the ponga tree where Rangi had tied the rope. Could it have come loose and floated off? No way. She remembers Rangi taking his time tying the rope. She already knows that he isn't the type of boy to make a silly mistake with a knot.

Could someone have taken it?

Possibly.

Whatever has happened, the boat is gone, Rangi is probably a prisoner and Katie is stuck up a river in the middle of the night with no way of getting back to the house and raising the alarm.

She knows she can't stay where she is. That won't help anyone. And if she doesn't get back, heaven knows what will happen to Rangi and the kiwis. It is up to her now and she isn't going to wimp out. She wipes her eyes with the back of her hand and takes a deep breath. She has to move.

But she doesn't, because just as she makes up her mind to move, she feels something behind her. There isn't any noise. She just senses a disturbance in the air. It's like waking up in the middle of the night and thinking someone is in your room.

The hairs on the back of her neck stand up so far she starts to shiver.

'Lost something?' asks a voice.

Katie jumps at the man's voice and a shrill scream escapes from her mouth. Before she even has time to turn round he grabs her arm so tight that his fingers dig right into her flesh. He turns her around so that they are looking at each other and he grins.

He is a really tall man and his face is covered in hair so that Katie can't tell where his moustache ends and his beard starts. All she can really see are his eyes. But she can smell him all right. He definitely hasn't showered in a long time. He smells of mansweat and sour milk and mouldy old socks. Probably of beer and cigarettes too.

The man is still grinning and Katie looks away so that she doesn't have to look at his horrible brown teeth.

'Your little friend ain't here, is he?'

Katie just looks at the man and shakes her

head. She is much too shocked to speak and is madly trying to work out how to get away. But it's impossible. Even if her arms were free, what can she do against this huge man? She can't even get close enough to kick him, and if she does, she just risks making him angry. Then what will he do?

Katie is at a loss and the man chuckles as he sees her slump in despair. He begins walking back through the bush pulling Katie along with him. He doesn't say anything else to her. He just holds on to her arm so tightly that she can feel his fingers bruising her skin.

As Katie is dragged back the way she has come her eyes are fixed on the rifle that is slung across the man's back. Now, she really is in trouble and she doesn't have a clue what to do.

She has never wanted her mum and dad more in her life.

CHAPTER 11

By now, Katie is so accustomed to the darkness of the bush that following the man is no problem at all for her. But it also means that her brain is raging inside her head trying to think of ways to get away, trying to think what will happen if she doesn't, trying not to think about what the men might do to her and Rangi and what will happen to the kiwis.

Her insides are tumbling all over the place and Katie feels like she is going to be sick.

As they get near to the shed, the dog starts barking and the man shouts something that Katie doesn't understand. The dog goes quiet and the door of the shed opens. Katie is dragged inside and pushed roughly into a corner where she lands with a thud and the back of her head hits one of the cages causing her to make an 'oomph' sound. The bird inside shuffles and Katie stifles a sob as she rubs her head. She has never been so frightened in her whole life and all she wants is her mum and dad.

A warm hand reaches for hers and Katie does cry a little as she clings on to it for dear life. Rangi squeezes her fingers and when Katie turns to him he gives her a wink. Whatever he has said about mana, Katie feels sure that he must be as frightened as she is and yet he is still being brave, whether he wants to admit it or not.

Katie thinks that if this is where she has to be, then she is glad that Rangi is with her.

She looks around and sees that the shed is now lit by an assortment of torches and lamps. Rangi is sitting cross-legged next to her on a few old sacks.

'Right, you pair,' says the man, who dragged Katie into the shed. 'Give us yer hands.'

They do as they are told and first Rangi's and then Katie's wrists are tied in front of them with rough rope.

'And be quiet!' he growls, before he walks

over to the table. A second man is already seated at the table and the two of them begin to talk in whispers. Katie has no doubt who they are talking about.

She still feels sick and tearful, but Rangi is watching her and she doesn't want to let him down. She tries to swallow away the really bad taste that is in her mouth and hiccoughs a little as she also swallows her sobs.

'You ok?' whispers Rangi, after checking that the men are not listening to them. Katie gives him a thumbs up and he smiles.

Katie knows that the two men at the table are obviously talking about her and Rangi because they keep looking over at them and pointing but she can't understand a word.

'I can't understand them,' she whispers to Rangi.

'They're speaking Maori.'

'Do you understand it?'

'Not every word,' he says, 'but enough.'

'What are they saying?'

'Wait.' Rangi shushes Katie while he listens, then he lies back on the sacks on his side so that the men can't see him talking.

'They're going to move us,' he whispers.

'Where to?'

'They haven't said exactly. They're packing up and moving out of here. They think our folks will come and look for us and find their shed. They're going to take us with them. I'm guessing we'll be going to the Ranges. To that other big shed in the bush.'

'What other big shed?'

'There's another shed, up in the Ranges. It's way bigger than this. It's where some fella tried to start a farm but as fast as he hacked away at the bush it grew back again. The shed's been there forever. It never gets used. It's a pretty hard ass tramp to get there, eh.'

'Have you been there?'

'Nah. It's a tough walk to not get a view at the end. Nothing to see but bush.'

'So, how do you know about it?'

'My ma and me take a hikoi up the mountain to pay our respects to our ancestors. Last time we were there we walked to the ridge and I eyeballed that old shed. It had been fixed up.'

'How was it fixed up?'

'I could see new metal shining in the sun straight in front of my eyes. Someone had patched up the old timber. Maybe with corrugated iron or something, but definitely metal.'

'Are you sure it was the shed and not a car or something?' asks Katie.

Rangi shakes his head. 'You can't get no trucks up onto that ridge,' he says. 'The only way is up a dirt track that comes off a logging road, but they would still have to walk the last section.'

'With all these cages?' asks Katie as she eyes those stacked around them.

'No-one would ever find them up there,' shrugs Rangi. 'And what I'm hearing from those men makes me think that's where it is.'

'Do they know that you understand them?'

Rangi shakes his head. 'That's our secret. But

listen, Kay-D.'

And Rangi very carefully describes the route that he took with his mum when they went up the mountain and exactly where he had seen the shed. 'You may need to find it on your own, Kay-D.'

Katie shivers at the thought.

'What are you talking about? You're frightening me, Rangi.'

'It's just best you know,' was all he says.

Something in his voice is frightening Katie.

'Will they hurt us, Rangi?'

'No, definitely not.'

Katie isn't sure if he knows that for certain, or if he is just saying that to keep her calm.

'Are you sure?'

He nods but looks away. He is listening to the men again.

'They just seem to be worried about getting caught. They asked me who knew we were here and I said no-one. I'm pretty sure they don't believe me. They're saying they don't want trouble. They're just poachers, Kay-D. They want to get away with the birds and get their money. We're nothing but a damn nuisance.'

'What will happen when we're moved?' Katie asks.

'They're taking us with them so we don't go and fetch the Police until they have got away. They have to take the cages somewhere tomorrow. So we're ok for now.'

'For now? What do you mean for now?'

Rangi motions Katie to lie down next to him.

'Listen, Kay-D. Those men won't let us go while there is any chance that we can give them away. But they won't keep us forever. They'll know that our whanau will stir up a fuss once they realize we're missing.'

'What's our whanau?'

'Family. Parents, aunties, cuzzies and that. What I'm telling you, Kay-D, is that we might not stay safe.'

The sick feeling is coming back again.

'You think they will hurt us – or kill us!'

'I think,' he says, 'that one of us must try and

get outta here. If we don't do something, all those birds will be gone. I think you must be the one to go.'

'Me!' Katie's voice squeaks and Rangi shushes her again.

'I can understand them,' he says, 'so I know what they're planning. It gives me an advantage and maybe there will be a chance for me to get away later. Right now I can distract them so you can get away.'

'How?'

'Look at them.'

Katie turns round to watch the two men. They are looking ever so slightly crazy and are jiggling around in their seats laughing and sucking on cigarettes. They have cans of beer in their hands and there is a big pile of empty cans in one of the corners of the shed. While Katie is watching, one of the men finishes his can, squashes it in his hand and throws the empty can on to the pile in the corner. Straight away he opens another can and when he tosses his head back to take a drink some of the beer spills down his face. He wipes his chin with his shirt sleeve. Katie pulls a face.

'What are they doing?' she whispers.

'Getting blotto, by the looks of it. If we're lucky they might crash out.'

'What if they don't?'

Rangi grins. 'Then I'll have me an epileptic fit.'

'You're an epileptic!'

'No, course not,' says Rangi. 'But one of the kids at school is and I know just how to make it look real.'

'So what do I do?'

'Listen,' says Rangi, 'I've got another plan.'

CHAPTER 12

So they sit quietly on the sacks and wait.

The men don't take any notice of the two children at all. They just carry on drinking beer and talking in their strange language while Rangi listens. Knowing that the men are only interested in getting the money for the birds has eased Katie's fears a little, but she still feels very, very frightened.

The men are being noisy, but not in a threatening way. They keep shouting things to each other and laughing but even though Katie can't understand them, she somehow doesn't feel that any of it is about her and Rangi. In fact, she gets the feeling the men have forgotten about them.

Katie knows that it must be getting really late because once she stops being terrified for her life, she realises that she is unbelievably tired. She lies down on the sacks next to Rangi with her bound wrists in front of her and listens to the snuffles and shuffles of the kiwi birds. In a strange way, the sounds are soothing and soon she falls sound asleep.

She is woken by someone nudging her with a sharp elbow. She is far too tired to get up and is about to say so when she feels a hand on her mouth. It smells like chocolate and pink marshmallow. She opens her eyes and finds herself looking straight into Rangi's brown ones. Everything that has happened seems to hit her brain at once and as panic overwhelms her she begins to struggle to a sitting position. Rangi holds her as firmly as he can with his bound hands and he nods as if to say, 'Yeah, that's right. It wasn't a dream. It's all real.'

Katie stiffens as the events of the previous afternoon come back to her and the reality of their situation sinks in. When she is still, Rangi removes his hand.

'Plan,' he mouths.

Katie nods and sits up straight. The shed is

still lit by the lanterns and she can see the two men slumped in their chairs with their heads on the table. They are both fast asleep and snoring loudly. One has his mouth open and there is a snail trail of drool sliding down his chin.

Rangi wriggles around so that his back is facing Katie and whispers, 'pocket,' and then, 'penknife'.

Katie hears the urgency in Rangi's whisper and knows that there is no time to think or question. This might be their only chance.

She reaches Rangi's pocket easily but because of the way he is sitting, his pocket is stretched taut and she can't manoeuvre her tied hands inside.

'Lie down,' she whispers. Rangi does as he is told and Katie also lies down so that she is facing his back. This way Katie is able to slide her hand into Rangi's back pocket and pull out his penknife.

As soon as she has it, Rangi sits up and shifts around so Katie can drop it into his hand. They are now facing each other. Rangi takes the penknife and cuts through Katie's rope in seconds. Katie rubs her sore wrists in relief and reaches for the penknife to free Rangi. He shakes his head.

'No, don't.'

Katie pauses in surprise.

'I have to stay,' he says.

'No, you can't. Why?'

'If I'm here, it may take them longer to notice you're gone. I need to stay with them, Kay-D. Find out where they go.'

'Rangi, no. I can't leave you here.'

'Don't argue, Kay-D. I know what I'm doing. Just get back and fetch help. The sooner you do that, the sooner me and the birds will be free.'

Katie places the knife on the ground in front of Rangi and sighs. 'Ok. But you better be right.'

'Put the penknife back and get the fish,' he whispers. 'Other pocket.'

Katie does as she is told and brings out a warm and rather soggy chocolate fish.

Rangi holds out the chocolate and quietly calls to the dog which is lying by the door of the shed. At first, the dog just looks at them, not interested at all until Rangi breaks off some of the chocolate and hands it to Katie. She throws it towards the dog who sniffs at it and then gobbles up the treat. Then, to her relief, the dog gets up and walks over to them wagging its tail.

'Now go,' says Rangi. 'Remember the plan.'

Katie throws her arms around Rangi and gives him a quick hug before she crawls to the shed door on her hands and knees. She holds her breath as she passes the snoring men and screws up her nose as she is bathed in alcohol fumes from their beery breath. Neither of them stirs. The dog stays next to Rangi, wagging his tale and gobbling up pieces of chocolate fish. Out of nowhere comes the thought that chocolate isn't very good for dogs but Katie dismisses it deciding that the welfare of Rangi and a shed full of kiwi birds is more important than possible future dog vomit.

Very carefully and quietly she opens the door and slips through, closing it gently behind her.

Can it really be this easy?

Rangi has warned her not to run the minute

she is outside in case it winds up the dog. That is just about the hardest thing in the world for Katie right now. Her gut is telling her to run like the wind and get out of there. Instead, she has to creep quietly through the bush back to where she had been before she was caught. She concentrates on every step and keeps reminding herself to stay calm.

Only when she is a good distance from the shed does she start to hurry and she is soon half running, half stumbling through the bush. The moon is high now and she finds it easy to see where she is going. Even so, she still manages to trip over something and land flat on her face in the ferns. But there is no time to moan and make a drama out of it. She is on her feet and off again before she has time to notice that she has scratched her face on something and her cheek is bleeding.

CHAPTER 13

It is only when she reaches the river that Katie starts
to cry. She is tired and relieved and scared and any
one of those things would have made the tears come.
All three bring a flood so that Katie bends over with
her hands on her knees and lets her tears splash onto
the ferns surrounding her feet.

Once she has started she isn't sure how she
will ever manage to stop. She hates herself for being
such a wuss but she can't help thinking about her
mum and dad and how mean she has been to them and
how much she wants them there right now. They
always manage to make things right. Katie swears to
herself that she will never behave so badly again if
only she can get back home. And just as she is
managing to gulp a few breaths and stem the flow of

tears, she thinks of the smashed iPad abandoned in her rucksack under the bed. She remembers how pleased her dad had looked when he gave it to her and Katie can't believe that she allowed it to fall to the floor so carelessly.

'Daddy, I'm sorry,' she gulps.

She has no idea exactly how long she has been standing there feeling sorry for herself, but she knows that it is far too long. None of this is going to help Rangi or the kiwis and she doesn't have time for anything else.

So, what next?

Stick to the plan Katie tells herself.

Rangi has told her not to even think of trying to fight her way through the bush. It would take too long and even if she could manage not to get lost, at some point she would have to cross the river. So without the boat, her only option is to get in the water and swim for it. That way she won't get lost and she can be quiet. Katie also knows from the movies that animals can't follow your scent in water so if they do let the dog out, he won't be able to find her.

But can she face it?

The water looks black and cold in the dark and Katie is not sure she has the courage to slide into it. She wonders what on earth is in that dark water and whether she is strong enough to swim all the way back to where they started the previous afternoon. It seemed like they had rowed for ages. Could she swim that far?

Well, there's only one way to find out, she thinks. She scrambles down to the water's edge and dips a foot into the water. Then pulls it straight back out. Boy, it's cold! In fact, it is freezing. And she has to get in there.

Katie keeps her clothes on in the hope that even when they are soaked they might give her a bit of warmth. She also keeps on her trainers because she is more afraid of standing on something in the water than the extra weight of the shoes. However, she does bend down and loosen the laces so that if they became really heavy, she can kick them off in the water.

Then she takes a deep breath and lowers herself into the water. The cold makes her gasp and it takes her a little while to realize that she is standing up. To her relief, she discovers that the channel is quite shallow with the water coming to just below her armpits.

It is too cold to stand still even if she had wanted to so Katie strikes out. She half swims, half wades through the water at quite a decent pace. The river bed is soft and she is walking on what feels like a grassy type of weed but she is still glad to have her trainers. Hurrying through the water is helping to keep her warm inside although it still feels icy against the skin of her arms and legs. All Katie can think of is getting back and getting help and she pushes on as fast as she can.

In fact, she is concentrating so hard on keeping moving that she doesn't register the sound at first. At least she hears it, but she doesn't actually recognize what it is. Then, as its insistent and steady note grows louder, she realizes that she can hear the thrum, thrum of a boat engine. It is coming from behind her and is getting louder as it gets nearer. Katie's heart begins to beat faster and with a huge effort, she forces her legs through the water to get herself over to the opposite bank where she clings to the long, wet grass for dear life, hiding in amongst the fronds and stalks as best she can.

She pulls the long, wet grass down over her head and freezing water drips down the back of her neck. In seconds the cold has crept into her bones and they begin to ache as if she has been swimming for hours.

It's too soon, she thinks, it's much too soon. Those men should have slept for hours.

The full moon is bright and Katie easily spots the boat as its pointed white nose pushes through the darkness. It's a small boat. Nothing like the size of the big one moored on the main river where she guesses it must be heading.

She can see one of the men at the front of the boat looking ahead as if he is the one steering and the second man is sitting beside him. Right at the back of the boat, she can see Rangi, sitting immobile, no doubt with his hands still tied.

Frolicking around the centre of the boat is the

beastly dog. It is bouncing around wagging its tail and looking very pleased with itself. Right at that moment, Katie would have been quite happy to see it bounce right off the edge of a very high cliff. But it isn't the poor dog's fault. No doubt it is only doing what it is trained to do. She imagines that poachers feel the same way about police dogs.

For flips sake, what is that?

Katie feels something smooth, long and very much a living thing slithering past her legs. Her breath catches in her throat at the shock and she screws up her eyes. She wills herself not to scream. It feels just like a snake. But New Zealand doesn't have any snakes. She remembers that from Google because it was one of the very few things that New Zealand had going for it. Even England has snakes. And Australia is positively infested with them.

Her eyes are screwed up so tightly that they are starting to ache and Katie tries her very best to relax and stay calm. She mustn't think about what is in the water because if she gets caught now both she and Rangi will be done for.

She opens her eyes to watch the boat pass and sees that it is pulling a barge stacked with the crates from the shed. There are plenty of them. She wants to know if they all have kiwis inside but she can't be sure. She also realizes that if the poachers have already managed to load their boat and set off, she must have taken longer than she thought to get this far.

She concentrates on the boat and watches as it passes so close she can see the whites of Rangi's eyes. She could swear that she saw the white of his teeth too. Just a flash as if he were giving her a little smile. And was that a tiny little nod of his head as if to say, it's ok, don't worry, Kay-D. Did he know she was there? How could he? And how could he be sitting up so proud and straight like a warrior? Not cowardly and scared like Katie feels.

Well, she could be a warrior too. Or at least someone that Rangi is proud to call a friend. She won't let him down.

The boat makes a swell in the water as it passes which ripples towards the bank and something bumps against Katie's shoulder. For a fraction of a second, she thinks it is the man again, although how he could have got from the boat to be right next to her in a second, she has no idea. Then she almost laughs because it is just part of a ponga log floating in the water.

A ponga.

Perfect.

In England, Katie's dad always used to watch the gardening programme on TV on Friday evenings. Katie thought it was really boring, especially as they didn't have a garden of their own, but sometimes she sat with her dad because she was too tired to do anything else after a week of school and homework. And Dad usually had a family bag of Maltesers to share. She remembered seeing the ponga trees on the telly because they were so expensive. Hundreds of pounds each and here they grew like, well, trees. But she also remembered the presenter planting them all by himself and saying how light they were.

And what had Rangi said? Pongas float. Even more perfect, thinks Katie.

She pulls the log in front of her and grabs hold of it with both hands. It is a bit slimy in places but she manages to get a good grip on the ridges of the trunk. She is really, truly cold now and her teeth are chattering so much she is giving herself a headache. She has to get moving so she kicks off from the bank and follows in the wake left by the boat.

She soon begins to feel the current tugging at the log and pulling her along. Ahead she can see a dark, open space as the stream opens up into the main river. Katie is so happy to have made it this far, she feels like giving a little whoop but she is too cold and wet and tired to even think about opening her mouth.

Once she has reached the main river, Katie finds that the water is deeper so that she is forced to swim rather than wade. She is so grateful for the ponga log that she names it Clark after Superman who always saved everyone.

The current pulls Katie along with sufficient force to keep her moving really fast. She hadn't noticed the current when they had rowed up the river, but then Rangi had done all the work and he had made it look so easy.

The good thing about it is that Katie doesn't have to work very hard to make good progress as Clark holds her up and the current pulls her along. Her brain is also thoroughly occupied thinking about Rangi and the kiwis and the poachers. So despite the cold, she is surprised to realise that she has traveled a long way and that she needs to look out for the little picnic table jetty which is where she has to get out of the water.

She knows that she will have to get right across the river to the far bank, so after she has been carried a bit further she begins to kick her legs to get across. It is definitely not pipsqueak because the river is three or four houses wide and the current is what Dad would call robust, meaning it wasn't going to make anything easy. And it doesn't help that she is seriously worn out. In fact, she is bone achingly tired.

She kicks as hard as she can towards the bank, at the same time watching out for Great Auntie Janet's house and ... oh no... there it is.

Katie kicks like mad totally soaking her head

in the process but it doesn't make any difference.

She sails straight past the house.

She lets go of the ponga log now and throws herself into her best front crawl, not caring how much noise and splashing she makes. She has never swum in a current before and it is the hardest swimming she has ever done. But inch by inch, Katie gets closer to the bank until with a final lunge the river bank is right there in front of her. She grabs handfuls of leaves and grass and begins to pull herself up. The bank is muddy and slippery, and by the time Katie has reached level ground she looks like she has emerged from a swamp. She is covered, in mud, weeds and goodness knows what else. But oh my giddy aunt, she is on dry land.

The only problem now is that she has gone a long way past Great Auntie Janet's house and she has no real idea how to get back there.

Not for the first time in the last twenty-four hours, Katie is completely and totally lost.

CHAPTER 14

As she sits dripping and shivering on the river bank
and trying to get her breath back Katie looks around.
She is more cold and tired than she had ever thought
possible, but now that she is away from the men and
their dog, she isn't so scared anymore. She is just
really anxious to get some help for Rangi. She doesn't
even care what Mum and Dad will say.

The bush is not so thick here, in fact, it looks
as though it has been cleared in places. Katie has no
idea where she is, so what's new, she just knows that
she has to keep moving. If only to try and warm
herself up.

Woof!

Oh give me a break, thinks Katie. Surely she
can't have got this far only to have walked right into

the hands of the poachers? Or even worse, the jaws of that stupid dog. She tries to get to her feet even though she has nowhere to go except back in the river but her legs have gone stiff from sitting down and before she knows what is happening she is knocked back by a solid mound of something very heavy and very hairy. Flat on her back and still soaking wet, Katie registers that she is underneath a great mountain of wet fur that is seriously trying to lick her to death.

'Gerroff!' is all she can manage but the dog takes no notice at all. Maybe it is a Maori speaking dog. She should have asked Rangi the word for stop.

When she finally manages to grab the dog's collar and hold him away from her, she is surprised to discover that he isn't actually a very big dog at all. Funny how you can get the wrong idea when you are flat on your back in the dark being smothered in doggie love, she thinks.

She can see that he is a small mongrel, probably only as high as her knee, if he would stand still for just one second. He has funny, floppy ears, wiry fur, a curly tail and right at this moment, he is just about the most gorgeous little dog she has ever set eyes on.

'Hello boy, hello.' Katie lets go of his collar and rubs his back until he starts to bounce around like Tigger. Katie thinks that there can be nothing quite so wonderful as finding a living, breathing friend when you are alone in a strange new world. Even if he is a four-legged one.

'Where have you come from?' she asks. But of course, he isn't a talking dog so he doesn't say.

Katie stops patting him to try and calm them both down.

'Come on then,' she says, 'let's go home. Come on, home.' She claps her hands and points towards the bush, praying that he isn't some sort of water dog who wants to swim home.

But he seems to get the message because with a yelp he runs off into the bush. Katie does her best to follow but even in the moonlight, she loses him straight away.

'Drat!'

At the sound of her voice he is back, licking

her hand and wagging his tail as if to say, 'come on then.'

The next time he disappears, Katie doesn't panic but keeps going and sure enough, he is soon back to check that she is still with him. The dear little dog keeps running off and coming back over and over until she spots a light up ahead and then she just focuses on dragging her tired legs towards it. One step after another until she is in front of a small, white, weatherboard cottage with a wrap-around verandah and a tangle of bicycles and muddy boots at the door.

The little dog is now barking up a frenzy and the door to the house is thrown open. Framed in the light that shines from inside is a great bear of a man. He fills the doorway so well that he blocks out most of the light and appears to Katie as nothing more than an outline. She can't make out his features very well as his face is shadowed, but she can see the muscles in his arms and a Maori tattoo across one shoulder. Katie takes a step back but the man takes one look at her before turning away and calling loudly over his shoulder.

'Mere! Mere!' And then some other words in a language that she doesn't understand.

As he turns back, Katie can see that his face is also tattooed with a pattern of lines and whorls that make him look like the men she has seen in pictures of jungle tribes. She gasps and holds her hands to her face with shock but the man doesn't seem to notice.

The huge Maori warrior of a man moves aside and indicates with a nod of his head that she should come inside.

He steps back into the house and the movement seems to let all the light out at once. For a minute Katie blinks and then in front of her is a lady. She is so beautiful that Katie finds herself staring. The lady is tall and slim, with long black hair hanging to her waist and lovely, familiar brown eyes.

Only afterwards did Katie think about how she must have looked, drenched from the river water and spattered with mud and weed fronds. But right now all she wants is to get warm and dry.

The woman rushes out and puts her arm around Katie to lead her inside while calling out instructions to the man, then muttering to Katie. Katie doesn't know what she is saying but her voice is very gentle and her words sound kind and comforting. At the very least she doesn't seem at all bothered to find a sodden creature from the swamp standing on her doorstep in the middle of nowhere. For her part, Katie just wishes she could understand what people are saying.

Katie hesitates for just a few seconds as her mum's voice warning her to stay away from strangers rings in her ears. But Katie is soaked and shivering and her freezing cold clothes are beginning to cling to her skin, heavy as chain mail, while her legs feel as if they are weighed down by cast iron boots. She can barely walk let alone run anywhere. And after all, Katie knows somehow that the great bear of a man with his patterned face is Rangi's dad and the beautiful lady is his mum. How could they be anyone else? So like Rangi and so close to Great Auntie Janet's house. Katie experiences a strange feeling enveloping her chest and filling her heart. At first, she thinks it's relief but with a flash of understanding, she recognises it as trust. She feels safe.

Katie's trainers are long gone by now, swept away by the currents of the river. How long will it take them to reach the sea, she wonders? How much will her mum shout when she finds out they are lost? Her bare feet leave a trail of wet footprints as she pads across the room and when she turns back, she can see wisps of bright green river weed in places where she has stepped.

She expects the inside of the house to look very different to all the houses she has visited in England. And this house is different, but it is also the same. It is different because the front door opens directly into one huge space with a vaulted ceiling like a church. There are wood-lined walls and floors, and a sitting room, dining room, and kitchen all tumbling together within one open space. It is the same because it has three well-worn sofas arranged around a slumbering log-burner. Each sofa is buried beneath an avalanche of cushions, soft toys, and children's books. She is in a family home that could be almost anywhere.

Rangi's dad has closed the front door and he watches as Rangi's mum indicates that Katie should sit down. He comes forward then and pulls a blanket from the back of one of the sofas and places it around Katie's shoulders with extraordinary tenderness for such a giant of a man. While Katie snuggles into the blanket, she watches Rangi's dad fiddle with the log burner, throwing on more wood and rattling a piece of metal so that the flames roar and a wall of heat rushes to claw at Katie's face.

In front of the fire lies a rag rug where the dog has already taken up residence in what is clearly his familiar spot. Katie pats him on the head and whispers thank you into one of his tatty ears. His tail thumps twice against the floor. It is only then that she is aware of three pairs of startled owl-like eyes staring at her from a large wooden table behind the sofas. The table is huge and has eight chairs arranged around it. Each chair is different from its neighbour in size, colour, and state of wear. One of the chairs looks as if it is leaning lop-sided onto a crutch, and as Katie peers more closely, she can see that there is indeed an extra piece of wood bound firmly to one of the existing legs. The sight of it makes her smile and as if this is a signal, the three sets of eyes return to what looks very much like homework.

Rangi's mum nods towards the children. 'They should be in bed but none of us could sleep. I told them if they don't sleep then they must do their schoolwork.'

Katie nods but her addled brain is unable to make any sense of what Mere is saying.

Beyond the table and the three studious, dark heads is the kitchen but from where she is sitting, Katie has to strain her neck to see it and right now, she is too tired and wet to care very much about the house. Except she does briefly marvel at the absence of separate rooms and wonders where the walls have gone and what is holding the roof up.

The man brings warm towels and another blanket, then he disappears while Katie undresses, dries herself and is wrapped like a parcel in a thick, warm blanket by Mere who places her back in front of the roaring log fire.

The beautiful lady talks to her all the time.

'I'm Mere,' she says, 'and who are you?'

'Katie.'

'Ok, Kay-D.' She says it just the way Rangi does and it makes Katie smile. 'You look like you've been for a swim, eh.'

She raises her eyebrows as she says it as if it is a great joke that anyone would want to go river swimming in the middle of the night.

'I have,' Katie agrees, 'I think there is a snake in there.'

'No snakes here, 'says Mere, 'it was probably an eel. You should have brought it back with you for our supper.'

'Oh yuck!' is all Katie can think of to say to that.

Mere laughs

'Is that an English accent?' she asks.

Katie nods. 'Are you Maori?'

'Aye, I am.'

Mere is rubbing Katie's hair with a towel.

'Are you hurt anywhere?'

Katie shakes her head. 'Just cold.'

Mere calls to the man again and he reappears with a steaming mug of something that smells milky and malty and very sweet.

'It's Milo,' says Mere, 'drink up.'

The man sits down on the settee and watches.

Katie hasn't tried Milo before but she likes it from the first sip. She is also beginning to feel her feet and fingers as they slowly thaw.

Katie looks from Mere to the man. 'Are you Rangi's mum and dad?' Even without a reply, Katie would have known that her guess was correct. They both start and Mere takes both of Katie's hands into hers. The man steps forward and crouches down in front of Katie.

'You've been with our boy? You know where he is?'

'You have to call the police,' Katie says to Mere, 'he's in terrible trouble.'

'Is he hurt?' asks Rangi's dad.

'What's happened?' asks Mere, 'what sort of trouble?'

'No, he's not hurt,' Katie explains. 'We went up the river in a boat to look at a shed. But two men came in a big boat, and they had a dog and… and…'

Katie starts to cry. Mere finds a box of tissues and pulls some out for Katie.

'…and mum thinks I'm still in bed,' Katie manages to hiccough between sobs.

'Where do you live?' Mere asks.

Katie opens her mouth to reply and then realizes that she didn't actually know. 'Great Auntie Janet's house,' is all she can think of to say. But that seems to be enough.

'You're the new English family,' nods Mere. 'When did you get here?'

'We only got here today and already I'm in the most awful trouble. I've even lost my trainers. Mum will kill me. But please, you must call the police,' Katie urges, 'I don't know what's happened to Rangi.'

'Kay-D, tell me everything,' says Mere. 'Start at the beginning.'

So Katie tells them everything. In fact, it was actually an amazingly short story to tell considering it had taken an afternoon and half the night to live through it. A meeting on the river bank, a row up river, a long wait in the bush, capture, escape and a long, cold swim in the dark until she was found by the little dog who was now curled up in front of the fire, twitching in his sleep and making little yipping noises as he dreamt.

Rangi's dad goes straight to the phone and Katie can hear him talking quickly, giving details, saying yes and no, sounding worried. It felt so good to have grown-ups in charge again.

'Hone's brother is a police officer,' explains Mere. 'He's already out looking for Rangi. He will come and talk to you and help us find him.'

'I'm sorry,' Katie starts to say, but Mere shushes her.

'No need,' she says. 'I know my boy only too well. He's always in one scrape after another. The important thing is that you got back here safely and you can help us. Now we must go and find him.'

Mere leaves Katie for a few minutes and returns with track pants, a warm top, and some thick socks. Katie puts them on guessing that they are Rangi's as she has to turn up the cuffs and ankles. She doesn't mind at all.

Rangi's dad calls her to the phone. She takes the receiver shyly expecting to talk to the police.

'Hello?' Was this small voice really hers?

'Darling, are you all right?'

'Mum!' She wants to cry again but Rangi's mum and dad are watching and she wants so much to be brave.

'Darling, are you all right? Really all right?'

Katie tells her mum that she is fine but that her trainers are lost, her new friend is a prisoner and she has been for a midnight swim in the river. Katie thinks her mum takes all of this quite calmly, all things considered. After Katie has finished her story, her mum says that she and Katie's dad will be right there.

And right then, there is nothing else in the world Katie wants more than to have a massive hug from her mum and dad. How could she ever have imagined that she hated them?

'I love you, Mum,' she says..

'I love you too, darling.'

CHAPTER 15

It actually takes Katie's mum a bit longer than 'right there' because, as she explained later, she had to go all the way down Great Auntie Janet's drive, along the public road, then all the way down Rangi's drive which apparently is even longer than Great Auntie Janet's.

Katie hears a knock on the door, some muffled words and then her mum rushes into the house and hugs her so tightly she can barely breathe. Katie hugs her mum back just as hard. Then her mum hugs Rangi's mum and she hugs Rangi's dad who Katie now knows is called Hone, and then she hugs Katie again. Then there is one of those predictable and almost scripted adult conversations. Thank you so much. Don't know what we would have done. So unlike our Katie. Dreadful way to meet.

Katie suddenly notices that her dad is missing.

'Where's dad?' Katie asks when there is a pause in the conversation.

'He's outside talking to a nice police officer,' says Katie's mum.

But he isn't. He is coming in the door with his arms opened wide for Katie to run into them. The police are close on his heels and for a short while, there is a general hubbub of greetings, exclamations, and questions. Finally, the younger children are tucked up in bed, everyone has a steaming mug of Milo and Katie is snuggled between her mum and dad.

Two police officers have arrived. One is a Maori who is as big and broad as Rangi's dad. When Hone gives the officer a huge bear hug and Mere kisses him on the cheek, Katie must have looked surprised. She has always been a little bit scared of the police in London. Especially if she sees them close up with their guns held against their bodies. This one was introduced to Katie and her parents as

Sergeant Nikau who is Hone's brother.

'Call me Uncle Nikau,' he tells Katie as he shakes her hand. She feels herself blushing at the thought. If Uncle Nikau notices, he doesn't say. He asks everyone to sit down and tell him what his naughty nephew has been up to this time.

The hour that follows is a bit of a blur. Katie is totally exhausted but her desire to help Rangi and the kiwi birds overcomes her need to sleep. The most important thing is to describe to the police exactly where Rangi was when she left him. Katie listens carefully to question after question and does her best to answer each one. Where had they gone? How? Why? When? What did they do when they got there? What did they see? What happened next? What did the men look like? What was in the cages? Are you sure Katie? Are you absolutely sure?

The more questions Katie answers, the more she realises just how stupid she and Rangi have been. She keeps looking up at her mum to try and say sorry but her mum just smiles and nods and sips her mug of Milo. Uncle Nikau's colleague takes notes and mumbles into his radio from time to time. Katie wonders if he is giving directions to the settler's hut but she has no way of knowing. The men seem to have a language all of their very own although Katie isn't sure that it is Maori. She recognises a lot of English words but the New Zealand accent, a smattering of Maori words and Katie's overwhelming tiredness make it difficult to follow. New Zealand is certainly taking some getting used to.

After answering what seems like enough questions to win Mastermind, Katie is left by the fire while the grown-ups talk over in the kitchen. She could have listened to what they were saying but keeping her eyes and ears open is a fight that she has no chance of winning.

Katie is woken by her mum after what feels like only a minute of sleep. She puts her arms around Katie and gives her a hug.

'What's happening, Mum?' Katie asks, in between two supernova yawns.

'It seems, darling, that you and your new friend...'

'Rangi.'

'You and Rangi, have managed to find yourselves a huge poaching operation.'

Katie knew that so she isn't as surprised as her mum seems to think she should be.

'That's what Rangi thought too. That's why we went.'

'Well, the police have known something about this for quite a while. Just by chance, a shipment of birds was intercepted at the port in Tauranga sometime last year. Since then the police have been trying to track the gang. Apparently, the police think that the gang has been making huge sums of money from trapping and selling kiwis to zoos and private collectors. Some are even being sold to the fashion industry for their feathers. They know that some of the gang have been trapping around here but they haven't been able to find out exactly where. They've had no luck at all. Until now of course. It looks as though you and Rangi have discovered their location.'

'Are we in trouble?'

Mum chuckles and hugs Katie tighter.

'You are in trouble with me for sneaking out of the house like that and frightening me half to death, but we'll discuss that later. If these men get caught, you'll have done a very good job and saved the lives of lots of precious birds. Right now though, we have to find them. And Rangi.'

'Do you think he's in real danger, Mum?'

Katie's mum gives Katie one of her looks. This was the 'I'm serious' look.

'He could be,' she says. 'Those men will be making a lot of money and they won't want to lose it. They won't like the fact that they have two witnesses either. On the other hand, it's not the sort of business that is known for any sort of violence to humans so we are all hoping for a good result.'

Katie shudders and her mum squeezes her again and rests her head against Katie's.

'Darling, at least you're safe and I thank God for that. We just want Rangi to be safe too.'

'What's going to happen?'

'The police are organizing a raid on the place that you found right now. There might be some clues that help them find Rangi and the men. How do you feel about helping them find it?'

'Will you and Dad come, Mum?' Katie asks. She's had enough of being brave. Right now, she just wants her mum and dad.

'Do you honestly think I'm going to let you out of my sight again,' replies mum putting on a shocked voice. 'Even if I have to ask one of the police officers to handcuff us together.'

'I'm sorry, Mum.'

'I know, darling. But some good has come from this. We just need to do all we can for Rangi. That means listening to the police and doing everything they say. Can you do that?'

'Yes, Mum.' For the first time in forever, Katie has no desire whatsoever to disobey her mum. For now, at least, her parents' word is law.

Just then Mere appears with a pair of Rangi's trainers. They are far too big but with the help of an extra pair of socks, Katie manages to secure them to her feet. Then Katie, her parents, and Rangi's parents are put into a police van. Katie has never been in a police vehicle before and really wants to enjoy it but she is much too tired and worried and just clings on to her mum with her eyes closed and her head nodding and jerking as sleep tries to take hold of her.

'I can hardly bear to think of you in that river in the dark,' says her mum. 'You were very brave and I want you to know that I am very proud of you. Even though you must promise me that you will never *ever* do anything like that again.'

'Oh, I promise, Mum,' and Katie means it from the very bottom of her heart.

By now she is quite used to not knowing where she is or where she is going next so she isn't worried when they bump along a narrow track that ends in a pot-holed car park filled with police cars. Behind the cars, Katie can see the glitter of water in the moonlight and as she climbs out of the car, she can smell the river.

They are taken to a boat ramp where three police boats are tied up and they are helped on board one of them. They are much bigger than Rangi's little blue rowboat and Katie settles at the back between her mum and dad. Suddenly she isn't so tired and is really keen to set off so that they can find Rangi and his little boat. She doesn't have long to wait and they are off before she knows it.

This trip up river is a walk in the park compared to swimming it. Mere is sitting opposite Katie and her parents and Hone leans forward to take her hand and murmur strange words to her. Katie looks questioningly at her mum.

'It's Te Reo Maori,' says Mum.

'It sounds beautiful,' Katie replies, 'I wish I understood it.'

As Katie stares at Rangi's parents, she can see that Mere has her eyes tightly closed and tears are slipping slowly down her face. Mere doesn't bother to wipe them away. Her hands are held firmly within Hone's and Mere leans her head against his shoulder. Although Katie has been scared and frightened, she hasn't given much thought at all to how Rangi's parents must be feeling. She was so relieved to be safe and back with her own parents, it hadn't occurred to her that Mere and Hone were still just as scared and just as frightened at the thought that their own child is still in danger.

As if sensing Katie's attention, Mere opens her eyes and looks into Katie's. Katie gives a weak smile and speaks the words without really thinking about them.

'Rangi has mana,' she says.

Mere and Hone both look at her. Mere smiles and Hone nods his head.

'Thank you, Kay-D,' they say in unison.

Then the boat slows and Katie is called to the front. They have arrived.

CHAPTER 16

Katie is asked to stand at the front of the boat and point out the way. They are much further up the river than Rangi's starting point and it takes no time at all to reach the inlet where the big boat had been moored. Katie spots it easily.

'There,' she points.

'Are you sure?' asks the police officer.

'Positive.' The channel would have been easy to recognize even in the dark but with dawn starting to lighten the sky, Katie has no trouble spotting it.

The police officer driving the boat slows the engine before cutting it completely. Then he fits some oars and quietly starts to row. With a strong police officer pulling them along, they are at Rangi's landing place in no time.

As they moor at Rangi's ponga tree, the other two boats slip silently past like ghosts on the water. Katie watches as they pull into the river bank up ahead and the police officers climb ashore. Everyone is silent.

They have been told to be as quiet as possible so they walk into the bush with careful steps trying not to rustle the bushes or dislodge anything. The police officers carry shaded torches and it is easy to follow the path that Rangi made earlier that night.

When they reach the flattened foliage where Rangi and Katie had lain, she stops and points to the shed. The bush and shed are only partially lit by the creeping dawn but the walls and roof of the shed make a funny reflection amongst the trees so it is easy to make out.

At this point, Katie and her mum are told to follow one of the police officers back to the boat and wait with Rangi's parents. They are ordered to stay well out of the way. Katie is a bit disappointed because she feels very safe with all the police officers but she has finally learned to do as she is told.

At least for tonight.

Rangi's mum had tried to argue about being made to wait in the boat but the police officers were really strict and told her that she stayed in the boat or she would be taken straight back home.

So she stayed in the boat.

When Katie gets back to the boat her mum takes her hand and holds on to her as they sit down with Hone, Mere, her dad, and a police officer.

They huddle in the boat waiting and listening. Katie remembers reading a book about the Second World War and how hard it was for the families left at home waiting for news and not knowing whether their loved ones were safe or not. Now she knows what that really feels like. Waiting is so, so hard.

Whatever is happening, it is something. The police radio crackles into life making everyone jump even though this is exactly what they are all waiting for. The police officer in the boat listens while five pairs of eyes watch. He doesn't seem to mind. Then they hear shouts from the bush and beams of torchlight are bobbing about in the trees.

The police officer does his mumbling on the radio thing for ages. Katie tries to listen but she is wasting her time. She will never be able to decipher the conversation in a million years. Her dad had told her once that he had tried flying lessons because he thought it would be a really great experience, but he gave up after two because he couldn't understand a word that was being said over the radio. Katie had always thought he quit far too easily. She would have loved a pilot for a dad. Imagine all those free flights. But finally she understands what he meant and now she has a dad who is going to be a farmer while Katie has inherited his radio deafness gene.

The mumbling stops and the police officer turns to speak to them in a normal voice. 'It's all clear. You can go.'

It would have been good if they had left the boat in an orderly fashion but that wouldn't be true. Instead they all pile out of the boat in an unruly heap not paying any attention to whether they might capsize the thing. They just want to be off the boat and at the shed as soon as humanly possible. Mere takes the lead, with Hone second and Katie and her mum and dad bringing up the rear. Katie's mum is still hanging on to Katie for dear life.

They are able to go right up to the shed and this time its doors are wide open and the place is lit up like a Christmas tree. They aren't allowed to actually go inside as it is a crime scene but they peer through the doorway.

Katie can't believe her eyes.

It is empty. Cleaned out, nothing there, all gone.

Whatever had been in there has disappeared along with the men, the dog, the kiwis and Rangi.

Katie thinks about the second boat and trailer that passed her while she was in the water.

Rangi's mum begins to cry.

'I'm so sorry,' says the police officer at the hut. He introduces himself as Dave and explains that he is the one in charge of the search for Rangi. He is older than Katie's dad, with short, grey hair and bushy grey eyebrows. He puts his arm around Katie to comfort her and pats Mere on the shoulder.

Neither of them responds to his touch. Mere is motionless while Katie stares at the empty hut. The table where the men had sat only hours before is wiped clean and faint rectangular marks amongst the dust are the only reminder of where the kiwi cages had stood. Even the stack of beer cans and the old sacks have been cleared away.

Katie's tired brain is finding it difficult to make sense of what she is seeing. When she was hiding in the narrow channel she had seen the small boat and trailer heading out towards the river where the bigger boat was moored, so logic told her that they had moved. It was the speed with which they have managed to move out that shocks her and the fact that they have not left a trace of their existence other than a few marks in the dust.

For a moment, Katie wonders whether it has all been a dream. Except that in the corner of the shed where Rangi and Katie had sat, she can see a single kiwi feather. Katie wants to bend down and pick it up. It looks soft and slightly curled and she imagines how it might feel in her hand.

Dave interrupts her thoughts. 'We'll get forensics in here straight away, but they have obviously cleared out and I'm not sure that we will get anything useful in a short time. They must have been prepared for discovery though.' He rubs his chin thoughtfully as he speaks. 'I don't see how they could have cleared out so quickly otherwise.'

'How *could* they have gone so quickly?' asks Katie's mum.

Dave indicates the shed in front of them. 'This is a professional operation and these boys are serious. They would have been prepared for discovery and your daughter said she saw the cages leaving on a barge. We'll do a wipe down but to be honest,' he shrugs 'we don't expect to find anything.'

'Are there any clues at all?' asks Katie's mum.

'Possibly,' he muses, 'the speed of the clear out and the fact that they've taken everything at short notice, and by water, suggests that they've got a second base not too far away. And it's also likely to be served by water. They took the boy by boat and they've moved the caged kiwis by boat. I'm betting on a backup space somewhere along this river. I wager that's where they will be and that's where they will have taken the boy.'

The small party traipses miserably back to their own boat.

Katie is suddenly so achingly tired that she could have dropped down right there in the bush and slept for England. Or should that be New Zealand? Instead, she follows the others wearily back to the boat listening to Mere crying and wondering what on earth she can do to help. Surely there must be something?

'We'll soon have you home,' says her mum, as they settle into the boat. Katie snuggles against her and closes her eyes. 'What you need is a good sleep,' says her mum. And that's exactly what she got.

Afterwards, Katie didn't even remember being carried up to bed in the arms of a police officer, which was just as well because she would have been *very* embarrassed. But jet lag, terror and a night in a cold, dark river had drained Katie of every last ounce of energy that she had. Even her worry over Rangi and the Kiwis was not enough to fight off sleep and at that moment, Katie would probably have slept through an earthquake.

CHAPTER 17

Hours later, Katie's ears pick up a noise that pulls her awake, although it takes her a little while to unstick her eyes which feel like they are glued together with sleep. She can hear her mum and dad's voices drifting through the open bedroom window and although she strains to hear what they are saying, their words are being drowned out by the most beautiful birdsong. Katie has no idea what the birds are, only that their song is the best she has ever heard. It is a long, double note that seems to be calling to Katie to 'get up, get up.'

So she does. Opening her eyes is proving to be hard work but the sun is shining and she wants to know what is happening. She clambers out of bed with a sense of urgency as if she were late for school and it is a test day. There is a pile of clean clothes at the end of her camp bed and Katie silently thanks her mum as she pulls them on.

She heads downstairs to try and find the kitchen in the hope that there will be orange juice and something to fill her grumbling tummy.

In England, Katie always enjoyed visiting the homes of her friends and she especially liked their kitchens. She loved the way that however strange and new a kitchen might be, it was always possible to find what you wanted. She loved it when a friend's parent told her to help herself to something and she would test herself by trying to find everything she needed without having to ask.

She didn't always succeed. Fridges that looked like cupboards could be a problem but Katie had learned to look for a glimmer of white enamel in the gap or even to listen for the faint hum of the motor. But on the whole, it is a game that Katie is good at and Great Auntie Janet's kitchen gives her the chance to play a new round. Kettle? In plain sight on the worktop. Cutlery? In the drawer underneath the kettle.

Mugs? Easy peasy. Hanging on hooks behind the kettle. Tea? In the wall cupboard above the kettle. Fridge? Obvious. No secret door to hide behind and inside there is a large carton of orange juice. Katie even manages to smile to herself as she walks out onto the wooden deck where she finds her mum and dad sitting side by side in a swing chair.

It is quite odd for Katie to see her mum and dad sitting down doing nothing together. In London, they might sometimes do nothing separately, but usually, when they were together, they were always doing something. Things like decorating, DIY, or at least planning what the next bit of doing would be. Today they are holding hands and staring at the view.

Katie is a bit nervous facing her mum and dad. She is ready for a major telling off. Her only thought is that at least they couldn't ground her. Much. They had done that when they brought her to New Zealand. If she thought about it, Katie realized that being taken to a strange, empty country was just about the biggest grounding an almost teenager could experience in her life. Short of being sent to prison. But Katie is pretty sure you had to commit some terrible crime to end up locked up at twelve and a half years old. Even so, she knows that she is well in the wrong for disappearing yesterday and causing so much trouble. She braces herself for the onslaught.

When the expected growling doesn't come, the shock almost shuts Katie up for the rest of the day. Her parents are both so very pleased to see her and make a space for her to sit between them.

'We didn't expect you to be up so early today. How are you feeling?' asks Katie's mum.

'Bit of a headache,' Katie admits.

'Bad enough for pills?'

She shakes her head. Swallowing pills is listed under 'too gross' in Katie's mental notebook of things to avoid in life. She has a few more things to add from yesterday's outing too. Like chasing poachers, swimming in cold rivers, getting lost in the New Zealand bush. Wow, it was getting to be a long list.

She takes a deep breath. 'About last night…' she begins.

Dad holds up his hand to stop her.

'Katie, you know that what you did yesterday was somewhat foolhardy, and not the sort of behaviour that we have come to expect from you.'

'But Dad,' Katie tries to interrupt but he stops her again.

'However, I don't think we need to discuss it further. I trust that you learned a useful lesson last night and I have every confidence that your behaviour will not be repeated.'

She nods and hangs her head. Dad usually takes a lot more than one or two words to tell her off but he never rants and raves like some parents. He just has this way of looking at her while he is talking, all narrow eyes and mouth in a straight line, so that she feels stupid and ashamed and totally unworthy.

'Now,' continues Dad, 'the police will be along a little later to talk to you again. It's vitally important, Katie, that you give them as much help as you can. Even the smallest clue might help them locate the boy. Quite frankly, you are their best hope right now.'

Katie nods. She can't bear to think of Rangi

held captive somewhere. She had half hoped that she would wake up to find that he was safe at home with his parents. Instead, he might be starved, or even beaten and what if… what if… No. She can't think like that. What she has to think about are clues.

Her fuddled, aching, useless, jet-lagged brain is no faster than a three-legged tortoise right now but something is niggling. There is something important. It must be something that Rangi said when they were in the boat.

Katie goes over everything in her head. Every detail, every word that was said. She tries to remember all of it. But however hard she screws up her eyes and concentrates, all she can see is Rangi and the dog and the men. And Rangi in the boat as it goes past her while she shivers against the river bank.

But she had done what he had told her to do. She had got away, kept out of sight and fetched help. It was, after all, the sensible thing to do. She was just too slow doing it, that was all. The men had left before Katie had even reached the main river.

But what if she could have done something to

help? Created a distraction so that he could get away? But what? Even safe between her parents in the broad light of day she had to admit to herself that there was nothing she could have done. She shuts her eyes and tries to replay the scenes from yesterday over and over again.

'Is your headache getting worse?' asks her mum.

Katie unscrews her eyes and shakes her head. She reaches for her dad's hand.

'Would they hurt him, Dad?'

'The police think not,' Dad replies. 'These men are basically businessmen. They are trying to make money. They certainly don't want the corpse of a teenage boy on their doorstep.'

Katie gasps.

'Andrew!' scolds her mum.

'Sorry honey,' says her dad, 'but the police don't think he will be seriously harmed. He is not a competitor. He is just a young boy that got in the way.'

Not seriously harmed. What's that supposed to

mean?

'They're villains, Andrew,' says Katie's mum, 'and you can't second guess them like that. You wouldn't be so blasé if it was Katie that was missing.'

'No, you're right,' says Katie's dad, 'and I apologise. They are evil men, I know that. But they are into making money, not kidnapping kids.'

'So why have they still got Rangi, Dad?' asks Katie.

Her dad shrugs.

'As the police have said, you kids just got in their way. Rangi is probably their insurance policy.'

'You mean like a hostage?'

'Exactly like a hostage. The police are hoping that as soon as the coast is clear they will dump him somewhere. He won't be a danger to them now they've moved on because he can't lead the police to them.'

But he already had.

Katie leapt up from the swinging chair causing it to jolt so violently that Katie's mum and dad clung to the arms.

'Katie!' chastises her mum.

'But he has!' she says. 'Mum, Dad, he has already found them!'

'What do you mean?' they ask in unison.

'Rangi told me there was another place. Another shed, almost identical to the one that he showed me.'

'Where, Katie?' asks Dad.

'Somewhere in the Ranges. Up a river or something. Where his great-grandfather is buried.'

'Are you sure about this?' ask her dad. His brow is furrowed into tram lines and his lips have almost disappeared.

'Positive. He told me he went there with his nanny and saw the shed. Honest, Dad.' She turns to her mum. 'I'm telling the truth.'

'I'll phone the police,' says her dad, and goes into the house to do just that.

Katie's mum gets up and hugs Katie. 'Well done, darling,' she says into her hair. 'We may find him after all.'

CHAPTER 18

Considering the fact that Great Auntie Janet's house is in the middle of nowhere, the police arrive in super quick time. Because the house stands high on a hill, Katie can see the cloud of dust thrown up by the wheels of the squad car long before it arrives at the door. She also sees the battered old truck that is following. While two police officers are still climbing from their car, the doors of the truck are flung open and Rangi's parents jump out.

In daylight, Hone's facial tattoo stands out sharply against his skin and Katie takes an involuntary step backward. She was used to seeing tattoos in London, on men and women, but somehow the coloured images on English legs and arms didn't seem as menacing as the one that covers Hone's face. When he stands still and silent, his face resembles a Maori carving so that when he blinks or speaks, the carving comes alive in a way that unnerves Katie.

He moves now and comes forward to greet Katie's parents by taking their hands and pressing his nose and forehead against those of her father's and then her mother's in the traditional hongi. Much more than a greeting, Katie knows from her long conversation in the shed with Rangi that the hongi is a welcome to join the local people. Kate thinks her dad receives the greeting with remarkable dignity but she can see from the way she blushes and flaps her hands that her mum is flustered and probably thinking, 'this doesn't happen at Marble Arch.' When Hone approaches Katie, she takes a breath to quell the fluttering she feels inside her and calmly presses her nose and forehead to Hone's.

'Tena koe,' says Hone, which is Maori for hello. Then he smiles and his face softens into the features of Rangi's dad. Katie lets out the breath that she didn't know she was holding and smiles back. She feels very proud that this huge Maori has welcomed her like this.

Mere repeats the formal greeting and follows up by giving Katie a huge hug.

'Thank you, Kay-D, thank you,' she says.

Katie can see that Mere's eyes are red and swollen and she feels terrible that Rangi is still missing.

'I'm sorry I didn't think of this last night,' Katie apologizes, 'it was only just now that I thought of it.'

Hone ruffles the hair on top of Katie's head and smiles.

'No worries, hine,' he says, 'better to remember now than not at all. You just needed a sleep, eh.'

Mere also nods and smiles at Katie and she thinks how lucky Rangi is to have such lovely parents.

'We would never find the place in the dark anyway Kay-D,' says Mere. 'Now is a good time, eh.'

Katie's mum and dad are rushing around finding chairs for everyone, some in cheap green plastic, the sort that belong to patio sets that crack and fade, a couple of stripy deck chairs that could have come straight off Brighton Beach and an old, ironwork armchair with a threadbare cushion that has seen much better days. It strikes Katie that in England mum would have been horrified at having to seat her guests on such a scruffy selection of chairs but here she doesn't seem to mind at all, and no-one else does either.

Maybe New Zealand is changing her already.

Katie's job is to bring out a tray filled with tea, coffee, orange juice and biscuits and then she is back in the Mastermind chair again as the questions start.

'Call me Dave' with the interesting eyebrows is in the question master's chair but he is such a grandpa with the way his eyes crinkle when he smiles that Katie doesn't feel at all worried. In fact, she tries really hard to impress him. She wants to do well. She explains about Rangi and his nanny and Mere nods.

'I know this place,' she says, 'I've been there many times to pay my respects to my ancestor. A carving stands there in recognition of his life and his work for my people.'

Dave spreads a map out on the deck.

'Can you show us where this place is?'

Mere kneels down to examine the map. A slight breeze lifts its corners and she reaches out with one hand to hold it flat while she traces the coloured contours with a finger. Katie can see that she is following the blue line of a river in an area of dark green.

'I can't pinpoint the exact spot,' she says apologetically, 'but it's around here, eh.' She prods the map confidently. 'I know I can take you right there.'

Dave confers with his colleague then nods to Mere. One of the police officers goes off to do the mumbling into the radio thing that Katie is now getting quite used to while Dave tells Mere and Hone to go home and get ready.

'We are ready,' is Mere's reply.

'But how will you find the shed?' Katie asks.

Everyone stops talking to look at her which makes her squirm just a little but even so, she speaks up bravely.

'Rangi said it wasn't easy to find,' she continues, 'but he explained to me exactly how he found it. If I was there, I think I could do the same.'

She says 'think' and not 'know' because she isn't one hundred percent sure that she can find the shed. She just knows that she wants to try. The thought of being left at home while everyone else is out searching is unbearable.

More conferring and mumbling follows and Katie sits quietly while she waits. Except that this time her mum and dad are in the middle of it. Then Dave gives Katie a thumbs up and it is all agreed. Mum will stay home as she isn't sure she is fit enough for a tramp in the bush and she doesn't want to slow them down. Katie will go with her dad, Mere, and Hone.

'Ok,' says Dave, 'cars are on their way, we'll meet them on the highway.'

If the reason for the journey wasn't quite so worrying, Katie might have totally loved the ride to the Ranges.

For starters, they were in a convoy of several

very smart police cars and vans, although you wouldn't have known because they were all plain clothes police cars. Not a blue light or neon strip in sight. This is a special unit, dad explains, used for undercover operations so the vehicles are top quality, smooth, powerful and air-conditioned.

Katie can tell that her dad is quite enjoying himself from the way he is asking lots of questions.

Katie sits in the back of the car between her dad and Mere, while Hone sits up front next to Rangi's Uncle Nikau. Katie thinks it is so cool that Rangi has an Uncle who is a policeman. She also thinks it is really cool that she is getting a ride in a real police car. Even if it isn't for a very good reason.

Because she still has no clear idea where she is, Katie also has no clear idea where they are going. Not that it matters, the police are very definitely in charge.

Katie knows that lots of kids at her old school don't like the police. They don't seem to trust them or maybe they are afraid they will get into trouble for something they may, or may not have done. Either way, it is not something that Katie had thought about before. All she knows now is that Uncle Nikau makes her feel very safe.

More than anything, Katie loves being back in a world where adults are in charge again. Stuck in the bush with Rangi had been the most terrifying experience of her life and she hates that he is still out there somewhere. She crosses the fingers of both hands and wishes with all her might that Rangi will be found safe and sound.

By now, they have been driving quite quickly along a highway for about half an hour.

'Breaking the speed limit,' whispers Katie's dad, with a satisfied smile, before they turn off onto a much narrower road. This one begins to twist and turn sharply as the cars climb rapidly and several times Katie has to swallow to make her ears pop.

The paddocks and fences that have lined the road for most of the journey have disappeared and now too the tarmac has given way to a gravel road. They are driving through native bush so thick that fronds and leaves are snatching at the car as they pass.

As the car climbs higher, the bush becomes thicker. All Katie can see are tree trunks, foliage, and ferns. She decides that as soon as she gets near a bookshop she is going to beg her mum to buy her a book so that she can find out the names of everything she is looking at. All she knows is that it is all incredibly beautiful and wild. Maybe she should learn to use a compass too. There are no road signs up here and even though she has been promised a mobile phone for her next birthday, she isn't sure that the signal will be too hot out in the middle of nowhere.

They drive through green tunnels of overhanging trees and branches and at times the road curves round open bends with steep drops to one side. At one point dad nudges Katie to look back and far below she can see the silver expanse of the ocean glittering in the distance. Then the car is thrown around another bend so sharply that she starts to feel a bit sick, so she has to concentrate on looking forwards which her mum always says is the best cure for queasiness.

'I didn't know we were so close to the sea,'

she says to her dad.

'Well, we're not so close right now, but the beach isn't too far from Great Auntie Janet's house. Fifteen minutes or so, in the car.'

'Can we go, Dad, when Rangi is safe?'

'It's the first thing we'll do.'

'And can we take Rangi?'

'We'll all come,' says Mere. 'We can show you where all the best kai moana is.'

'What's that?' Katie asks.

'Good seafood,' replies Hone, turning around in his seat. 'Best in the Bay.'

'I might even buy myself a little boat,' muses Katie's dad.

Oh my days, thinks Katie. Imagine her dad buying a boat. What was going on now? Her workaholic dad is in grave danger of turning into a human being.

'Great idea, Dad,' she says, with a grin.

The car slows as the gravel road of lumps and bumps becomes rougher and when the last tiny stones roll away to clatter down the mountainside, they bounce along on a track of deep, rutted mud. Fortunately, the surface is dry so they don't get stuck but it is an uncomfortable journey.

The car in front has thrown up a huge cloud of dust and Katie begins to feel as if they are driving through a heavy cloud even though she knows that the sun is shining and the sky is blue.

'Thank goodness for four-wheel drive,' says her dad, 'otherwise we'd be in the ditch.'

Katie doesn't like the sound of that at all and clutches onto the back of the seat in front of her. She is desperate to ask if they are nearly there yet, but a cliché is the last thing she wants to be. She compromises by asking in a different way. 'How much further?' she asks Mere.

'Not far. But then we must walk.'

Walking is something Katie doesn't mind. At least she will be in control of her own legs and not at the mercy of four wheels and Nikau's impersonation of a rally driver.

The track ends in a small clearing. There is hardly enough room to park the cars let alone turn them around and Katie hopes they won't have to leave in a hurry. The doors of the various vehicles open up to let out a collection of very scary looking men but when Katie says as much, Nikau tells her they are all police officers. To Katie, they look like something from Star Wars. They are dressed in bulky, black clothes, heavy boots, helmets with visors and they are carrying guns.

Katie nudges her dad. 'Guns!'

She has never seen so many guns close up before. They look very big and very, very scary. Her heart thuds a bit then because it makes her realise that this is all totally real. At the same time though, the police and their guns make her feel really safe. Like she is a member of the good gang or something. She is very glad to be on their side. Maybe that's what people mean when they talk about being on the right side of the law.

Katie and her dad stand to one side with Rangi's parents while the men are given their orders by Dave. Then Katie's group of four are briefed separately. Their orders are very clear. Katie and

Mere's job is to pinpoint the exact location of the hut. If they are successful they are to back quietly away and point it out to the police. The police will storm the hut and civilians are most definitely not allowed anywhere near it while the operation is in progress. This is for their own safety. They are to return to the parked cars and wait for news. The journey is to be made in silence if at all possible.

Dave asks if there are any questions but there aren't any. They are ready for the off.

CHAPTER 19

During the car journey, Katie can see that Mere was holding something on her lap that looked like a fluffy coat or jacket. As she leaves the car she shakes out a long feather cloak which, despite the promise of a long, hot walk, she drapes around her shoulders.

'That's a beautiful korowai,' says Nikau.

Mere nods her thanks and without so much as a glance at the others, she moves to the front of the group without seeming to move at all. Katie was expecting her to be nervous or upset but there is no sign of any nerves. The rest of the assorted bunch are fidgeting and shuffling their feet, anxious to get started, but if Mere has any emotions, she is keeping them to herself. Katie finds herself hopping from foot to foot until a sharp, 'Katie!' from her dad makes her stop.

The sun is already warming the tops of their heads and the sky is so blue, Katie finds herself squinting against the bright sunlight. A faint breeze stirs the soft feathers draping the shoulders of Mere's korowai so that it looks to Katie like a living, breathing thing. Mere tosses back her long, black hair and turns to face the sun. Katie watches as Mere lifts her face to its warmth and closes her eyes as if she were drawing strength from its rays of heat and brightness.

Despite her impatience to get moving, Katie finds herself watching Mere. She isn't really sure why. Maybe it is the way she looks in her beautiful feather cloak. Maybe it is because she seems so calm even though her son is missing. Maybe it is just that after her recent experience, she is glad to let the adults take control. Whatever the reason, at that moment, Mere seems ancient and other-worldly, and Katie feels a shiver of something she doesn't understand.

Right then, it is as if Katie's own will has disappeared and she will follow Mere to the ends of the earth even though she has no idea why. The respectful manner of the police as they wait in silence behind Mere makes Katie think that perhaps they feel the same way.

Katie thinks about Rangi's explanation of mana.

Katie had not truly understood what Rangi was saying until this moment, but now she does. Mere has mana, by the bucket load.

Katie listens as Mere mutters in Maori.

'It's a karakia,' Hone whispers in Katie's ear. 'A prayer. She's asking her ancestors for guidance.'

Mere finishes with 'amine' the Maori amen, and several of the police officers join in. Too shy to speak out loud, Katie murmurs her own amine. She has no memory of ever being taken to a Church in London, even at Christmas. School assemblies and nativity plays were the extent of her praying and hymn singing until now. And right now, the karakia seems to be a good way to start their journey. Even though Katie had not understood the words, she guesses from what Hone has said that Mere is asking her ancestors to watch over them and to bring her boy safely home.

Mere opens her eyes and without hesitation, begins to move forward into the dense bush. Katie springs after her leaving her dad and the police officers having to hurry to catch up. There is no obvious track to follow but Mere moves with a steady, confidence, winding her way around trees and shrubs without stumbling or pausing.

Despite the order from the police to move as quietly as possible, Mere moves at a brisk pace. Katie has read about people who do amazing things when their loved ones are hurt or in trouble, like lifting cars single-handedly when their child is trapped beneath. She thinks about these stories now, as Mere forges ahead. Even the police officers are starting to puff a bit. Katie pities them dressed in their heavy gear. It must be like hiking inside a portable sauna.

Katie can smell the heat of the day rising, and she is soon hot and puffing herself, but whenever Katie's dad taps her back to check on her progress she turns and gives him a thumbs up. Under no circumstances is she going to be sent back. She has never thought of herself as an outdoorsy sort of person but she is enjoying the challenge of keeping up with the adults. In any case, this is about finding Rangi and helping the kiwi birds, and if it causes Katie a few blisters then so be it.

She takes deep breaths of the clear morning air and her nose is filled with the scent of something mossy and primeval. The bush is already very much awake and while the tramping boots of the police officers will have frightened away any animals, the tree canopy is alive with whistles and chirrups as the birds and insects go about their business.

The further they walk, the denser and thicker the bush becomes. The myriad of greens and browns are muted by the shade except now and again a startling shaft of sunlight pierces the branches of the trees and illuminates a grove of ferns or a tangle of supplejack. Feeling thirsty, Katie slows her step near to one particularly convoluted mass of vines and tears off a tip as Rangi has taught her. She sucks on the refreshing juicy stem.

As the air continues to warm and the humidity rises, Katie notices that the path is becoming steeper and more rugged. In places, it is steep enough to need handholds of branches or tufts of ferns to help climb up the rocky path. Occasionally her dad gives her a helping hand to haul her over a particularly large rock, or to steady her where the ground is slippery. Katie's T-shirt is so wet it is sticking to her back and her feet feel hot and sweaty inside her shoes.

Katie feels for Great Auntie Janet's carving which still hangs around her neck. It seems to make her feel better and even though she is still desperately worried about Rangi, Katie glances down at the pendant and hopes that she might be able to keep it. Its whorls and patterns intrigue her and she is beginning to realise that there is more to this country than she had originally thought.

The steepness of their route has slowed the pace of the search party and Katie can hear the sound of water nearby as it rushes down the mountainside. Despite the supplejack, Katie is overwhelmed with thirst and tugs at the sleeve of her dad's damp shirt ready to ask for water.

Before he can respond, Mere raises her hand to signal that they should stop.

They have arrived.

Despite the heat and the beautiful feather korowai, Katie thinks Mere looks cool and calm as she stands tall in the forest. Behind them, the police team and the two fathers begin sliding silently back into the bush until Mere and Katie appear to be quite alone. Heading up a pack of armed police officers would not be a good look.

Mere and Katie are to go to the memorial stone as if they are relatives paying their respects. Just in case they are being watched. Once they are there, Katie's job is to try and spot the shed, or at least the direction of it. If she manages to identify it, she will let the police know so that they can move in and raid it.

Katie and Mere move forward eagerly now that their journey is almost at an end. Although they don't speak, Katie guesses that they are both thinking about Rangi and how close they might be to him.

The shaded light of the bush begins to brighten, the foliage becomes crisper and patches of sky are peeping through the tree canopy. Without warning, Katie and Mere emerge into the open and find themselves standing near the banks of a rushing, frothy river. Katie can see it is not deep this high up, probably more of a mountain stream than anything, but there are clusters of rocks and boulders which make the water hurry and scurry in a tangle of waves and foam.

They are high enough for the breeze to find them again and Katie lifts the hair from the back of her head to let it cool her neck.

Out from beneath the tree canopy the ground is covered with a sparse, scrubby grass and huge vistas are visible around them. Mountains stretch as far as Katie can see and the land is folded between the peaks with a green softness that stirs her heart. She has never seen anything so beautiful. She feels as if she is on top of the world.

Mere takes Katie's hand and without the thick undergrowth to hinder their progress, they are able to walk side by side. Their footsteps are muffled by the breeze and all Katie can hear are the receding forest sounds; the birdsong, the trilling cicadas, and the rush and gurgle of fresh water tumbling over rocks.

At the edge of the stream, Mere kneels to drink from a cupped hand and indicates that Katie should do the same. Katie sucks thirstily at the icy water. It is the sweetest water she has ever tasted.

The noise of the water is loud enough to cover the sound of their voices where they crouch and Mere bends towards Katie. 'Just up here,' she says.

They scramble a little further up the hill to a place where the ground levels and reveals a wide, circular pool many metres across. On one side of the pool, nearest to them is an enormous stone carving. It is twice as tall as Mere, a solid, grey block that must have once been a quite ordinary, uninteresting lump of nothing. Now it is like something that should be in an art gallery in London. It is awesome. Carved all over with patterns and faces, it is hard to tell where one bit finishes and another starts. Dotted amongst the faces are eyes decorated with blazing blue stones that glitter in the sunshine making Katie feel as if they are watching her.

'Their eyes,' whispers Katie, feeling a little intimidated by their glare.

'That is paua shell,' explains Mere. 'I think in England you call it abalone.'

Katie shakes her head, not quite understanding. There is not much call for seashells in London.

'Do crabs live in it?' she asks.

'No, it's a snail. A sea snail. Very good to eat. But like your little kiwi birds, even the paua get poached.'

'For the eyes?'

'They get poached because people like to eat them. It's considered a great delicacy,' she adds, as she sees Katie grimace at the thought of eating a salty ocean snail. 'But,' continues Mere, 'the discarded shells are polished and used in carvings to represent the eyes of our ancestors. They are like the stars gazing down from the night sky.'

Once Katie sees the frightening eyes as stars

she is awestruck and loves the carving so much she could have stayed staring at it for a very long time. It is an unwanted sense of urgency tugging at her heart that makes her move. They have a job to do and Mere is urging her forward.

Rangi has to be found. And the kiwi birds must be released.

From the monument, they continue to follow the gushing water up the hill. Katie is soon hot and thirsty again and is panting hard as they clamber upwards. Without the tree canopy for protection, the sun is already beating down and Katie is glad of the cap that her dad had insisted she wore. Occasionally, her weary legs stumble and she begins to feel as if her feet are not her own. She feels quite envious as Mere continues her climb without pausing for breath.

Mere stops abruptly and points ahead, 'Ponga,' she says.

Katie looks at where Mere is pointing and in front of her, she sees the beautiful, iconic silver fern. Its straight trunk looks furry as if it were wrapped in its very own korowai, and it's branched leaves arch from the top like an unfurled, and very fluffy umbrella.

'It's beautiful,' murmurs Katie.

'It's a powerful symbol of inspiration for Maori,' explains Mere. 'In the moonlight, the underside of the leaves glows silver to guide us through the native forest. Now, let it guide us to my son.'

Katie glances at Mere, wanting to tell her how relieved she feels to have found this place, and how glad she is that Rangi had been clever enough to tell her how to find it. Mere nods at Katie as if she is feeling it too. They walk towards the ponga together and pause beneath its canopy where the young, green fronds push their unfurled spikes up to the sky, while the old, brown ones sag towards the ground. It isn't a tall tree and some of the fronds tickle the back of Katie's neck. She turns with determination towards the sun and walks straight ahead, squinting against the bright light.

This is the place. She knows without a doubt. It has to be here. She can *feel* it.

They are now standing on a broad ridge that stretches away in front of them. The ridge is dotted with vegetation, small pongas and stunted bushes but as the ground rolls away on either side, the blanket of bush smothers the ground so completely it is impossible to see very much at all beyond the roof of multi-coloured leaves.

Surrounding them are dozens of neighbouring ridges which twist and turn in all directions. Katie feels that she is looking at the roof of the world.

She checks to make sure that she is standing facing the sun and forces her eyes to relax beneath the peak of her cap. Rangi had described the shed as old and rusty. It had probably been standing since colonial times. Only the new patches in the corroded metal will stand out. They are small, perhaps no more than slivers. Katie begins to scan the vista systematically. Mere is silent beside her. All Katie needs is the tiniest glimpse.

Katie mumbles a mild curse at her stupid London eyes. She wants eyes that can see more than a mass of greens against a sparkling, blue sky. She feels as if the world is out of focus and she screws up her face in concentration.

'Keep looking,' murmurs Mere at her shoulder. 'Let the bush show you what shouldn't be there. Mauri te pono. Believe in yourself.'

Katie scans the area ahead of her again. This time she lets her whole face relax. Her eyes drift across the carpet of foliage. Then they stop.

There!

A glint of silver between the trees.

Katie walks on a few more steps, just to be sure, but there is no doubt that she is looking at something that nature despises. Metal. Katie squeezes Mere's hand and points. Mere sees it too and tightens her grip in response.

'Ka rawe, Katie. Awesome. Well done,' she whispers.

As previously agreed with Nikau, as soon as they see the shed, they turn to retrace their steps. No noise, no fuss, this is the end for them. There is no more that they can do as instructions have been made very clear to them by Nikau. As soon as the shed is spotted, they are to leave. They cannot be exposed to the danger of armed poachers.

They do as they have been told and turn to make the long trek back to the cars. When they reach the cover of the bush, they stop while Mere explains to the police the exact position of the shed. Then Hone and Katie's dad appear with one of the police officers who escorts them back the way they have come.

Mere had paused just once on the way back. At the ancestral stone she laid the palm of her hand against its surface then bowed her head and murmured softly in Maori. Katie bowed her head too and although she didn't understand the words, she heard Mere's prayers to her ancestors asking them to continue watching over a lost and beloved son and to deliver him safely back to his family.

'Ake, ake, ake amine,' she had finished. Then she turned and took Katie's hand.

'We are done, Katie. Let's go home.'

Katie had assumed that Mere meant her home because the words reminded Katie that she didn't have a home in New Zealand. There was a room in Great Auntie Janet's house that she could sleep in but it wasn't really her room. The memories of her old London bedroom bounced around inside her head and in every one there was a strange girl inhabiting the space that used to belong to Katie.

'That's done too,' murmured Katie under her breath. Because being in this foreign place had made her realise more than anything that everything had changed. Whatever happens from now on, her old life is gone. The flat, her school, London, England, everything is finished. Even if she makes it back when she is older, everything she had known, and everything she had been would be gone or changed forever. With this thought came an overwhelming sadness. As Katie walked, her tears fell silent and unseen into the undergrowth.

CHAPTER 20

Going down is always faster than going up and it doesn't take long for Katie, Mere and the two dads to get back to the cars. A police officer offers to drive everyone home but the collective 'No!' is loud and unanimous.

Katie's dad puts his arm around her shoulder and squeezes gently. 'You did well, Katie. I'm really proud of you.'

Katie shrugs but doesn't say anything. She is pleased that her dad is proud of her, but she can't shrug off her feelings as easily as she can dismiss a compliment. The sadness that she had felt on the mountain hangs around her shoulders like Mere's korowai. Maybe she just needs to know that Rangi is safe and she will feel better.

Katie's legs are aching and she finds a large boulder that is smooth and flat enough for her to climb on to. Sandwiches and soft drinks appear and Katie samples her first bottle of L&P or Lemon and Paeroa which she finds too sweet and swaps for water. She also has a Colby cheese and pickle sandwich, which tastes just like cheddar, followed by some Whittaker's chocolate which she likes so much she saves the wrapper so that she can ask for it again.

There is nothing for any of them to do but wait. So they wait. And wait. Now and again the police radio crackles as if it is about to share some important news and everyone hurries over to the cars to listen intensively. Mostly, the words are too distorted for Katie to understand and the police officer has to translate, but mostly the chatter is about other jobs and incidents and nothing to do with Rangi and the kiwi catchers at all. After a while, tiredness begins to nag at Katie and her dad suggests she lies down in the back of the police car and closes her eyes for a minute.

As she stands, her dad points to Great Auntie

Janet's carving.

'What's that?'

Katie flushes. 'I found it in the house. I just really liked it. It was ok to take it, wasn't it?'

He shrugs. 'Of course.' Katie knows that he has no interest in jewelry.

Mere peers at the carving and leans forward to stroke it with a forefinger.

'That's very special,' she says.

'Is it? Why?' Katie asks.

'This is something that would have been carved for one particular person. I would need to take a really good look at it to find out more. Maybe even take it to one of the elders at the marae.'

Katie's hand closes around the carving at the thought of losing it for even a short while.

Mere notices the gesture and smiles. 'You are attached to it?'

'I can't explain. I just like it,'

'Then it was meant to come to you,' says Mere. 'Objects like this have mana. They always find their way to their true owners.'

Katie likes that idea. There is a trace of a smile on her face as she curls up on the back seat of the squad car and closes her eyes. Her last thought is to wonder if she can take the carving with her, if she ever goes home.

A sharp rap on the car door wakes Katie with a start and brings everyone to attention. Mere's hand flies to her mouth. Dave is there looking red-faced and anxious but smiling. Really smiling in a way that shows all of his teeth and crinkles his eyes. The police officer winds down the car window.

'Dave?'

'All good,' says Dave, 'He's out, he's safe.'

Katie shrieks, Mere cries, Hone says no-one knows what and Katie's dad slaps everyone on the back, even Katie, unnecessarily hard. They all tumble out of the car in a muddle of knees and elbows, all ready to rush somewhere though Katie doesn't know where. But before they have gone more than a few paces, a huddle of black padding and space helmets comes out from the trees. Right in the middle of them, Katie can see the men from the shed in their dirty jeans and T-shirts with their wrists handcuffed behind their backs. They still look scary and Katie is very happy to see them pushed quickly into the back of a police van and driven away.

Katie stands watching the van depart in a cloud of dust when she is interrupted by a rather offended voice.

'Took you long enough, eh.'

Katie turns and right in front of her is Rangi's cheeky face smudged with dirt, but with the grin intact and his hair still sticking out in every direction.

Then he disappears from view under a tangle of hugs and kisses and tears.

When he eventually emerges Katie can't help teasing him. 'You look like you've been plugged into the National Grid.'

He smiles and tries to flatten his hair but it refuses to listen.

'Don't worry, it suits you,' she says.

'You cool?' he asks.

'Yes, are you?'

'No sweat.'

'I'm so sorry, Rangi,' Katie apologizes.

'What for?'

'For taking so long to get the clue.'

'What clue?'

'About the shed.'

'How come you're here then?'

'Well, I did get it in the end. But not till this morning. I fell asleep.'

'Well, least you didn't freak like some girls might and go screaming through the bush getting caught.'

At this he does a very fair impression of a young girl running round in circles, waving her arms and mopping her brow squeaking, 'help me, help me!'

Katie doubles over with laughter.

'I'm still sorry.'

'Wanna know something?' he asks.

'Yes.'

'There was no clue.'

'But the story about the tin shed…' Katie begins.

'Just a story. I wasn't thinking about giving

clues 'cos I wasn't thinking about getting caught.'

'Oh,' was all she could think of to say.

'Good job anyway, mate,' he says.

Katie smiles and Rangi gives her a quick hug. Actually, it isn't much more than a quick squeeze but it would do.

'Ok folks,' says Dave coming over, 'we're all done here. Let's go home.'

'Got anything to eat?' asks Rangi.

CHAPTER 21

The drive back to Great Auntie Janet's goes really fast. Everyone wants to hear what happened to Rangi while he wants to know how every single switch in the police car works. He even manages to persuade Nikau to give a quick blast of the siren and blue lights which Katie thinks could have got Nikau into a bit of trouble, so it was good of him to risk it.

Katie thinks that Rangi really enjoys telling his story. He makes everything sound very ordinary, even though it couldn't possibly have been. He says he was very scared when he was taken away from the first shed in case his hunch was wrong and he got taken somewhere completely different.

'I just knew we would go to the Ranges,' he says, 'because the sheds looked the same, eh.'

'Were they the same inside?' Katie asks.

'Pretty much,' he says. 'Mostly stacks of cages and stacks of beer. Good job them guys like their beer, eh?'

Rangi seems so excited about what he has seen that Katie can't believe that he was actually kidnapped at the time. He doesn't seem bothered at all. In fact, Katie thinks he is quite proud of himself.

'Weren't you scared about what they might do to you?'

'A bit,' he shrugs, 'but I reckoned if they were going to do me in they would have done it there in the bush where no-one would find me. Once I was in that boat I was leaving traces.'

'Traces?' Katie queries.

'You know, hair and skin and DNA and stuff.'

'You watch too much TV,' says Mere, ruffling his hair.

'So what happened after you had gone off in the boat?' Katie asks.

'We got out at the boat ramp and went in a car up to the Ranges. Course,' he says proudly, 'I didn't let on that I knew where we were going.'

'But you would have seen where you were going.'

'No way. They blindfolded me before we turned off the highway but I knew it was the Ranges we were headed to. I could tell by the way the road was going up.'

'So, what happened when you got there?'

'I just acted like I was lost. Thought if they knew I could find the place again they might not be too happy, eh? They were still a bit blotto I reckon.'

'Did they say anything to you?' Hone asks.

'Nah. Just ignored me. Stuck me on a mattress in the corner tied to a pipe. Know how the dog feels now.'

They all laugh.

'Weren't you even a little bit scared?' Katie asks again.

'Not so much,' he shrugs, 'to be honest, I fell asleep.'

'What?' Katie can hardly believe her ears. 'You were a hostage in a poachers den and you *fell asleep!'*

'They took no notice of me. Boy, I was whacked. Guy needs his sleep.'

Hone and Mere laugh again and even dad joins in but Katie is still flabbergasted. She has been so worried about Rangi the whole time he was missing and most of that time he was taking a nap! Then she remembers that she too had fallen asleep and begins to feel a little bit embarrassed.

'Then when I woke up,' Rangi continues, 'those blokes were out of it. Reckoned they'd helped themselves to a few too many cans. I made loads of noise trying to get untied but they didn't move a muscle.'

'So when did they wake up?' Katie asks.

'When the police walked in.'

'They just walked in?'

'Yea, that was so cool. They just looked through the windows, saw the guys asleep and walked right in. Them blokes were still snoring. What a wake-up call, eh? Open your eyes to find the squad in your bedroom. It was so awesome. Wouldn't mind seeing that again.'

'Don't you even think about it, boy, or you're grounded till you're old enough to vote,' scolds Mere.

Rangi just grins as if he knows his mum better than to worry about that threat happening. He just burrows into her arms and that's where he stays all the way home.

Later that evening, Dave comes round to Great Auntie Janet's house to talk about what has happened and to ask Katie more questions for his report. She is getting to know him quite well now and thinks that she will miss him, except Mum and Dad invite him to dinner the following weekend and he accepts at once. He also says he will bring his granddaughter if that is ok because she is about Katie's age. The best news is that he tells Katie she is invited to see the kiwis being released back into the wild and he wonders if his granddaughter can come too.

Course she can.

Katie's mum and dad stay up late that night talking for hours. Katie lies in bed, tossing and turning and listening to the murmur of their serious voices. In the end, she gets bored and finally falls asleep.

Next morning at breakfast both Katie's parents look very serious. She thinks it is time for her big telling off but boy, has she got that wrong. They manage to surprise her yet again.

'Katie,' her mum begins, 'Dad and I have something that we want to discuss with you.'

Discuss, not tell, that was a good start, thinks Katie.

'We need to have a serious talk,' her mum continues.

Not so good.

'If it's about me running off like that, Mum, I am truly sorry and I promise I will never, ever do it again,' interrupts Katie. 'I really have learned my lesson. It was horrible and I never want to go through anything like it again. Ever.'

'It's not about that,' says Mum shaking her head, 'that's all been done and dusted. It's more about the bigger picture.'

Katie's mum takes a deep breath. 'When your

dad and I decided to come and live here, one of the reasons was that we believed New Zealand would be a safe place for all of us to live. Somewhere where we would all have a better quality of life, away from the dangers of city life, away from crime.'

'And poachers…' Katie interrupts.

'And where we could all be happy,' continues her mum. 'That means you too, Katie. This running away business has really made us realise just how unhappy you are about coming here. It was so out of character for you to go running off like that. It's not what we wanted for you at all,' says Mum.

'Done and dusted, Mum,' Katie reminds her.

'Done and dusted in terms of the event, yes. Not done and dusted when we consider the reasons why you did it.'

'Mum, I didn't mean to…'

'I know Katie,' she interrupts, 'but you did something totally out of character. I know how upset you were at leaving England, but your dad and I thought we knew best. I have to be honest and say that we didn't give your opinion enough attention.'

Is she apologizing to me? thinks Katie.

'We both apologise for that,' says Dad.

Wow. This is a first.

'What we are trying to say,' says Mum, 'is that Dad and I are willing to reconsider whether this is really the best place for us.'

'What we mean,' says Dad, 'is that if you are really that unhappy about being here, then we would consider returning to England.'

'But our old flat is sold, isn't it?' Katie asks.

'Yes it is,' says her mum, 'we would have to find somewhere else to live.'

'And would you both have to go back to your jobs.'

'Probably,' says Dad, 'unless we decided to downsize and live a little more frugally.'

Frugal. Doesn't that mean living like you are really poor or something?

Katie thinks about what they were saying. She thinks about England and her mum and dad hardly ever being around. She thinks about them always busy and never doing anything together and then she pictures them on the swinging chair that morning. Both of them just being there. Together. At the same time.

And making a space for Katie to be there with them.

She thinks about watching the kiwis being released. The ones that she has helped save. And then she thinks of Rangi, of what a great friend he is going to be. And she sneakily thinks of all the really great adventures that they are bound to have together.

'So, what do you think, honey?' Dad's voice interrupts her thoughts.

She looks from her mum to her dad and notices their English worry lines crisscrossing their foreheads. She notices how they both have their fists clenched on the table.

Katie looks at her parents. And then she smiles.

It is a really happy smile.

'So, do you want to go back home, Katie?' asks her mum.

'No WAY!!' Katie shouts.

Her mum and dad look at each other, a little surprised maybe, but they both shrug as if to say, that's that then.

'Are you sure, honey?' asks Dad, 'do you need some time to think?'

Katie shakes her head. This, she was really, really sure about. And she is still smiling as she replies, 'This is my home now and I'm not leaving it. I've got my kiwis to see. And besides,' she adds, 'New Zealand rocks!'

Printed in Poland
by Amazon Fulfillment
Poland Sp. z o.o., Wrocław